D1553724

SAM FOSTER

ALPHA MALE

A TALE OF THE BATTLE OF COMMERCE

2002 · Fithian Press, Santa Barbara, California

Copyright © 2002 by Sam Foster
All rights reserved
Printed in the United States of America

Fourth Printing

This is a work of fiction. Characters, companies, organizations and agencies in this novel are either the product of the author's imagination or, if real, used fictitiously without any intent to describe their actual conduct.

Published by Fithian Press
A division of Daniel and Daniel, Publishers, Inc.
Post Office Box 1525
Santa Barbara, CA 93102
www.danielpublishing.com

LIBRARY OF CONGRESS CATALOGING-IN-PUBLICATION DATA
Foster, Sam, (date)
  Alpha male : a tale of the battle of commerce / by Sam Foster.
    p. cm.
  ISBN 1-56474-397-7 (pbk. / alk. paper)
  1. Real estate agents—Fiction. 2. Professional ethics—Fiction.
I. Title.
  PS3606.O77 A47 2002
  813'.6—dc21
                                   2001005488

ALPHA MALE

I have labored, for my entire business career, in the practical and pragmatic world of "the deal." But two of the people I love most are creative. This work is dedicated to them, my son with a BA in Creative Writing, and my wife, whose degree and business are in illustration and design. Between them they cajoled and encouraged that there was enough creative juice in this old business stone to wring out a pretty good story.

ALPHA MALE

CHAPTER I

Consent

THE DISPLAY READ 5:19. Jack Kendrick watched it flash to 5:20. He finally pulled his arm from under the warmth of the duvet and toggled the switch from "Alarm." No reason to disturb Lorna. Also no chance he'd fall back to sleep in the next ten minutes. He'd been awake, off and on for the last couple of hours—since the moon moved past the eaves and started to shine into the window. Now, close to setting, it beamed in with enough intensity to read by. Well maybe, with glasses and twenty-point type he could.

But it wasn't the moon that kept him awake and he knew it. He'd thought through today two dozen times. Just how firm would Harkness be? More important, how firm will I be, he thought to himself.

The click of the solenoid in the Mr. Coffee was sharp as a shot from the bathroom. He usually didn't hear it. It was 5:25. Just a couple of minutes more. God, it felt good here—warm and snugly next to Lorna—and safe too. They can't get you when you're under the covers.

The sweet pungent odor of the espresso roast drifted under his nose. 5:30. That's it, time to get up. Jack patted Lorna's soft hip pressed into his back, turned down the cover and slipped out. He grabbed the thick white terrycloth robe from the bedpost and pulled it on before the cool braced him, but his bare feet were cold against the marble floor when he walked into the bathroom. The moon was so bright he could make out the pastel stripes on the Caleca mug Lorna sat by the pot. He filled the mug with coffee, turned and walked across the bedroom and out the French doors into the backyard.

The moon setting into the Pacific presented a stunning display. The water was like glass and the moonlight paved a path that invited him for a stroll. Venus' usual brilliance was dimmed. Below him red-tiled rooftops paved the South Bay. Those near to the mercury vapor street lamps glistened in their warm orange glow.

Spanish pavers led across the trimmed grass to a redwood gazebo surrounded by bougainvillea. Jack's destination was the hot tub in the center. Steam drifting from the edges of the cover gave mute evidence to the warmth below. He sipped the coffee as he trod firmly across the slick tiles. Jack sat the mug on the bench, pushed the cover off the back of the tub, shed his robe, retrieved his coffee and slid in.

Waking early is never easy, but this kinda takes the sting out, he thought as he hooked his elbows over the edge of the jacuzzi, slowly stretched his spine into an upward arch and lowered his head over the back of the tub. When he looked back up, it was at a heavenly vision.

Lorna stood gloriously naked framed in the doorway and lit by the moon. Jack stared at his wife, entranced as she strode slowly toward him. Tall as she was, just inches below his own six feet, her legs seemed to rise forever. Graceful athletic legs. Her waist was still slim, and the slight curve to her belly and the weight of her breast beginning to lose the struggle with gravity, gave her all the more allure. No child this, but still stunningly sexy. In the three years they'd been married he never bored of seeing her like this, and suspected he never would. Her long hair, which looked black at this distance, was pulled onto her head with a claw.

"Join you or are you pondering the day's battle?"

"I am, but you can. And quick before Ian sees you and gets Oedipal on me."

She arched a toe into the water, and then, seeming satisfied, walked in and took the two steps across the waist-deep water to him.

"The odds of a fifteen-year-old boy being up at this hour seemed small enough to risk it." She smiled. "The show was just for you, did you like it?" She sat down on the bench, water up to her neck, and wedged herself under his arm.

"Silly girl." Jack pulled her tight to him.

They sat saying nothing but watching the moon slowly sinking and listening to the surf a mile away.

Jack inhaled sharply as she laid her hand on his leg and then arched her palm and slowly dragged her nails up his thigh. The mug made a thud as he dropped it to the ground behind them.

"The moon will set in about two minutes. It will be pitch-black from then 'til dawn. If we're quiet it won't matter who else is up."

He dropped his arm around her and lazily caressed her shoulder for a moment and then stopped. "I said you could join me, but I also said I was pondering the day's battles."

Her hand went flat on his leg and stopped moving. "Serious?"

"Yeah. Can we save it for tonight?"

"I'll be lucky if you stay up long enough to sing 'Auld Lang Syne'."

"I managed to stay up last year."

"You weren't up at five-thirty that morning."

Jack noticed that the house was beginning to be a silhouette against the sky. "Sorry, honey, I don't want to ruin the evening. I'll stay up to see in the New Year. Promise."

The mass of her hair was lying against his neck. "Seems to me you weren't asleep much last night. Wanna tell?"

"Harkness called yesterday and insisted I meet him at ten o'clock today." He was still for a moment. "Emphasis on insisted."

"Not going to be congratulations for running the best office he had this year, and maybe giving his number-one manager a big bonus." She moved away just enough to look at him.

Jack didn't look back. "He wants the year to be even better. Four hundred thousand dollars better."

She continued to look.

"I'm holding a file open that Harkness wants closed so we can book the income this year. I don't sign off and close it, the money just sits there and won't get into this year's books."

"Why not close it and make him happy?"

"I'm not sure it's legal." Jack now returned her gaze. "Donaldson hit another long ball; leased two floors of a Century City office building. Check arrived yesterday."

"And?"

"And the disclosure statements show he represented the Landlord. And that he also represented the Tenant. Landlord knows he was representing both of them, his consent form is right there, but I'm not sure the Tenant knows. Consent form isn't there."

"So?"

"So, my darling, California law says the principals in a real estate transaction have a right to know who's their agent and exactly whose interest that agent represents. Quaint concept having to do with trust, I understand."

"Sarcasm is not one of your more endearing traits."

"Sorry, honey. I guess I'm getting my game face on. Didn't mean to point it at you."

She pulled her hand from the water and patted his shoulder. "It's okay, no harm, no foul. So what's Donaldson got to say about all this?"

"Mr. Donaldson wasn't around yesterday. Seems he spent the day on a plane to Hawaii. I left a message on his voice mail saying, 'No consent form, no check.'"

"So what's Harkness going to do, force you to sign the file?"

"He can't do that. He can insist, but he can't force me to do anything."

"So what is he going to do?"

"That's what I've been pondering half the night. Whatever he does, he'll do it in his usual pushy way."

The house was now clearly silhouetted by the lightening sky. The sun would be up soon.

Jack pulled her toward him until her face was next to his and then kissed her briefly. "It's time to leave this paradise, put on my battle gear and go find out."

He stood up dripping. Lorna looked up at him with a mischievous smile and then held out her hand. Jack took it and pulled her up then stepped back so he could take in the sight of her. Steam rising off her body into the predawn light gave Lorna a surreal halo. Jack pulled her close and let his hands fall until they were caressing her naked bottom. The warmth of her was almost overwhelming. A small shudder started in his belly and ran up his spine. He raised his hands to Lorna's shoulders and pushed her away until she came into focus. "Whatever it is, Lorna, don't worry. I can take care of all of us."

"I have no worries on that score, honey. It's *you* I'm worried about."

Jack picked up his terrycloth robe, smiled and handed it to her. "You wear it. Some things are just too good to share."

* * *

"I'm tired of all this ethical shit," Harkness spat. "We close the books for the year as of the end of business today. Today, Jack. Not next week; not tomorrow; today. And the Metropolitan transaction along with its four hundred thousand of revenue is going to show on those books. This year's books. The 1991 books. I am not about to let some pissant manager with a prissy attitude about complete files stop that. Have I made myself clear, Jack?"

Harkness made it sound like an insult rather than his name. He'd made the same point several times during the last hour. But this time he didn't make any attempt at being polite. He was abrupt and forceful. The end of Harkness' patience was in sight, and Jack's tenure as manager of the Beverly Hills office of Southern California Commercial Properties along with it. Jack understood his problem and he thought he understood Harkness' too.

"How's your annual bonus figured?" Jack asked. "Percentage of the gross plus a percentage of the net? Maybe two of the one and ten of the other? This time of year almost everything is net after the salesman gets his half. I sign, your bonus goes up, what, twenty-five, maybe thirty thousand dollars?"

"Sign, asshole!" Harkness demanded.

"Fuck you! And don't call me asshole. Being my boss only buys you just so much, and it doesn't cover that."

"It buys me the right to fire your ass!"

"For what?" Jack felt the corners of his mouth pull back sharply forming a sardonic smile. "Keeping So Cal Commercial out of a lawsuit? You know damn good and well Donaldson lied to those guys."

"You don't know shit," Harkness spat. "Ted Donaldson has been the star of this office a whole lot longer than you've been managing it. He's doin' deals. You're doin' shit."

"Okay, so he didn't lie to them." Jack didn't try to hide the sarcasm. "So he told them straight up that while he was representing them he also just happened to be representing their landlord. They just haven't gotten around to signing the consent form yet. It's just a paperwork thing."

"Sign the file!"

"And your star salesman, Donaldson, just happened to take vacation at year end. Never a thought in his mind you might want the deal booked over the objection of your 'prissy,' was it, manager. Tell you what. There's the phone. You call 'em. Right now. They agree to the dual representation, fine. We'll fax over a consent form. They sign; I sign."

Harkness stared at him. All the adrenaline and upset gone

from his face. No frown; no smile. Just staring. Silence filled the room. When Harkness spoke he did so slowly and evenly.

"Jack, I guess I didn't make myself clear. When I said, 'You are going to sign off the file, and you're going to do it now,' what I meant was that the manager of the office was going to sign off the file and do it now. File approval is the responsibility of the manager of the office. And the manager of this office is going to sign off this file, now." Harkness shoved the signature page of the file across the table toward Jack, took a pen from his pocket, pulled the cap off, and offered it to him. "So Jack, tell me, are you still the manager of the office?"

CHAPTER 2

Time To Wake Up Lizzy

THE LIGHT from the top of the canyon had diluted the inky black-
ness just enough to separate the tone framed by the window from
the rest of the bedroom. A mockingbird made a first tremulous
attempt at its morning song.

Liz wasn't sure if it was that which awoke her or if it was the
warm mass of Tommy's engorged cock nestled into the crack of
her ass. Why do men always wake up with a hard-on, Liz wondered. Now's not the time to wonder about that. Now's the time to
appreciate it.

She reached a hand behind her back, and stroked her fingertips along Tommy's stomach until she could feel the depression
running down the middle of his abdominal. Slowly she walked her
fingers further down his belly until her nails were twirling the curls
of his pubic hair. Tommy pushed his groin even closer to her ass,
but the rhythmic pattern of his breathing didn't change. Liz enjoyed the journey down Tommy's body. When she reached the
base of his prick she slid her fingers around it until her nails were
scraping across the wrinkled skin that covered his balls. His rock-
hard cock twitched as she turned her wrist and gripped it with her
fingers. Or tried to.

He inhaled spasmodically and the slow rhythm of his breathing changed. She could tell he was awake. "Tommy, time to wake

up Lizzy," she instructed. His breath warmed her back as he kissed her between the shoulder blades, and then licked down her spine, one vertebrae at a time. With his hands on her shoulders he slid further down into the bed until his cock slipped from her grasp.

Tommy's moist breath filled her with warmth as his tongue worked its way between her cheeks, and when he licked across her asshole it was Liz's turn to inhale sharply. "Tommy, Tommy, baby. Suck my ass. Oh, God that's good. Now suck Lizzy good."

When his forehead forced the backs of her thighs to part, Liz raised one leg over his head and turned onto her back. Tommy rose onto his knees, kissed the inside of her thighs, and licked his way up until Liz could feel his breath on her pussy.

"Tommy, stop teasing and suck me off God damn it!" Liz grabbed at Tom's thick curls, and pulled his head until it was just where she wanted it, with Tommy attached to her clit like a suckling puppy. As he licked, Liz squirmed in languorous bliss, her hand wandering from his hair up her belly to her breasts. Her desire rose slowly as Tommy continued—rose until everything disappeared except the heat in her cunt. No thought. Only her cunt. And then it swept over her and she shook from her shoulder to her knees with delirium and release. "Tommy, Tommy, Tommy! Oh, sweet Jesus! Ohhhhh!"

Liz saw Tommy's head and shoulders silhouetted in the grey light of the bedroom windows. He kneeled over her with what she presumed was a smile on his face. "Baby, you are the best," she whispered as control gradually returned. "You've earned a little reward. Let's find someplace to put that big hard prick of yours." Liz grabbed his shoulders and forced him over and sideways, onto his back. "Would you like to stick this into Lizzy, baby?" Liz placed her hand around as much of his cock as she could grab, and while he nodded she threw her leg across his body, and filled herself with Tommy's talent.

* * *

Liz came out of the dressing room ready to go. The dove gray suit only hinted at the curves underneath, except for her legs. Too proud of her long legs to hide them, she'd had the tailor raise the hemline of the skirt to just above her knees, and she wore three-inch heels. The heels put her eyeball to eyeball with most of those tough guys. Negotiation was a man's game, and being able to go toe-to-toe with them and give as good as she got was the first rule she'd learned. The second was never, never let them know you're hurt. Her height helped with the one. She didn't need help with the other.

When she walked into the kitchen, Tommy stood at the counter in his robe, cracking eggs into a mixing bowl. "Hi, honey. You look good. Not like a girl who just got ravished, but very good. Got time for an omelet?"

"Sorry, sweetie. Gotta run. Are you taking Audrey to school or is Isabel going to do it?"

"I'll do it, babe," he frowned. "No staff meeting this morning so I can drift in whenever I get there. Are you going to be home in time to see her for dinner?"

"Tommy, don't start. You can handle her, and if not, that's what Isabel's paid to do."

Tommy said nothing as he beat a few spoonfuls of water into the eggs. Silence echoed off the tile.

"Tommy, let's not ruin a nice start to the day. For the last five years that bastard has been running my ass around town and taking credit for everything I do. No more. That's it. He's pushed me as far as I'll go."

He set down the bowl and turned as though to speak.

"We've talked about all of this," Liz continued. "I need to show him. Him and the whole damn market."

"What about us, Liz? What about Audrey and me?"

"I'll stay as late as I need to beat that bastard." She could feel the heat rise to her face. "I'm the one, Tommy. Me. I've been doing it all while Paul Jensen fished and played cowboy and took the credit. Now I'm free of him and everyone is looking to see which of us will rise and which will fall. I'm going to beat that prick into the ground." Liz pulled a ceramic mug out of the cabinet—its bottom was twice the circumference of its top—and walked over to the coffeepot. "And I'll do whatever it takes to do it. Whatever it takes."

After filling her cup with steaming black coffee, she walked away; her heels played staccato notes on the tile. She knew Tommy watched the way she moved. She called back over her shoulder, "I'll try to be home to tuck her in. I'll try."

* * *

The tires squealed as Liz snatched at the wheel to pull the Lexus back from the drunk bumps. As a rule, she found steering with her knees easy but when she'd grabbed at the ringing phone and dropped the eyebrow pencil she'd drifted a bit. She had to let go of the phone and take the wheel in hand or risk sideswiping the eighteen wheeler running beside her. Son-of-a-bitch had been glued there for the last two miles. Hadn't the bastard ever seen legs before?

"Peterson here," she barked into the phone as she fought to regain control.

"Hold for Mr. Cornblatt, please," the restrained voice insisted.

Liz waited through the click of telephone switches.

"Lizzy darling, are we having a bad morning?"

"Cornie, what a pleasant surprise. What's got you calling first thing in the morning?"

"Well, sweetie, to start off, it's mid-morning here in New York. And secondly, I wanted you to know that all that work you and Paul have done for me over the years is about to pay off. That's a call you shouldn't mind getting, even if I did catch you putting on your makeup in the car."

"Just finishing the eyes," Liz admitted. "It's such a waste of time just driving from the house to the office. I can do both at once."

"But can you do them and not get in a wreck? That's the question."

"I'm a girl with lots of talents. Don't worry about me."

"You go, girl," he tittered.

"Tell me more about all my work paying off. Is America's largest distributor of consumer electronics finally getting that new warehouse you've been talking about forever?"

"You got it," Cornie answered. "We're going to need about two hundred thousand square feet near the Ontario Airport."

"How soon?" Liz tried to keep the excitement from her voice.

"Typical of Vance Electronics—we're going to want it ASAP. I can't get out there until the first of June. When I arrive, I'll want to find an existing building. We won't have time to build one. Send me a current list of every warehouse over two hundred thousand square feet that's available."

"Will do." And then Liz added, "Cornie, one little thing for you to know. Nothing to concern yourself about. But I just want to let you know that you won't be seeing Paul on this. He and I aren't working together anymore."

"You and Paul split up the partnership, huh?" There was silence, and then he added. "That's your affair, Liz. We'll do fine together. Just get me what I want."

CHAPTER 3

Life's a Beach

LOOKING WEST from the stoplight at Pacific Coast Highway, Jack could see the Santa Monica Bay from Palos Verdes to Point Dume. Across the intersection the terrain undulated down a series of dunes, each dropping lower than the last, until a mile away the broad white sandy expanse of beach met the Pacific Ocean.

In February when the Santa Ana winds blow, Los Angeles is the most beautiful city in the world, Jack thought. Where else could you have an eighty-degree day at the beach in a city ringed by snowcapped mountains, and the sky clear blue, seasoned with little white puffy clouds. And the day would end with a stunning sunset, Jack knew, because when the Santa Anas cleared the smog out of the basin, they pushed it all out over the Pacific where it could refract and color the lengthening rays of the setting sun into a paint box of oranges, browns and purples. God, I love LA.

He was snatched back from his reverie by the jerking of the big K-5 Blazer as the transmission unsteadily engaged. Jack smiled, and without raising his head from the high seat back, looked over his left shoulder at his frowning son. "Ian," Jack said, "you still need to practice the clutch part, don't you?"

"Yeah, that's why they call it a learner's permit." Ian shifted smoothly into second gear as they crossed the intersection and headed down the hill into the high priced residential area of

Manhattan Beach. "I'm learning. But I've got five whole weeks before my birthday and my driver's test. Think I'll make it?"

"I'm not sure if I'm more scared you will or you won't, but if you don't back off that little Beamer a car length or so, you're going to be the only kid in your class with points on your license before you ever get it."

Ian's mouth turned up in a playful smile. "Not so! Jamie Escobar got hit with Exhibition of Speed last week, and he just got his learner's in January." But he touched the brake lightly and added more space between the Blazer and the BMW. "Where are we going again?"

"To Mike Grazlyn's," Jack answered. "He lives on the Strand between 17th and 18th. Follow 2nd to the beach, and turn right on Ocean. He's got one of those houses that goes all the way through the block and faces onto the Strand."

"Okay," Ian answered. "But we're never going to find a place to park. Every surfer and bronze goddess in LA is gonna be down here today."

"Mike said all we'd have to do is pull in parallel behind his garage."

As Ian pulled away from the stop sign at Valley Blvd., the transmission engaged smoothly, and father and son both indulged small smiles.

As they neared the beach Ian asked, "Do I know Mr. Grazlyn?"

"You've met him but I doubt you'll remember. He started out with So Cal Commercial twelve or thirteen years ago. He was straight out of college. Linebacker at SC."

Ian's eyes lit up.

"He was a smart kid," Jack continued, "and very driven. I helped him with his first couple of deals. Then we worked together around Beverly Hills and Century City for a few years. But he hasn't been there for seven or eight years now. You were a little kid the last time you met him."

"So where'd he go?" Ian asked.

"He joined American Corporate Real Estate, ACRE is what everyone calls it," Jack answered. "When he joined them he went to the east end of the LA Basin, around the Ontario Airport, and he started working industrial land. It's been a very hot market. Mike's done well. Made a lot of money."

As Ian negotiated the right turn onto Ocean, he slowed to let two teenage girls in bikinis and on roller blades glide past them toward the Strand. Jack stared. Both were blondes with hair flowing past their shoulders. Their bikinis were day-glo yellow; like neon signs that flashed, "Great tits, aren't they?" They were, Jack agreed. He adjusted his sunglasses to conceal his rapt concentration.

"So do I tell Lorna you drool at teenagers," Ian asked, "or do we discuss what kinda car I get again?"

Jack continued to stare, but openly now. "Whatever you can buy for a thousand dollars. Not a dime more. She already knows I drool at teenagers."

"That's right. I forgot. That's how you met her." Ian grinned.

"She's not that young, God damn it." Jack feigned indignation. "Half a man's age plus seven. That's the rule for propriety in these things. We make it."

"Maybe, but she doesn't quite fit the Wicked Stepmother image." Ian turned his attention back to his driving.

"Lord, I raised an irreverent child with no respect for his elders," Jack complained to no one in particular.

"So why are we seeing your old friend Mike, besides letting me practice my driving and you practice your drooling?"

"Because, my son, I want his help getting a job. I don't get a new job, the car's on hold, and you're still on a bicycle."

"In that case I'm glad to help," Ian said. "You okay with all this, Dad?"

"I'm not sure, Ian, but it doesn't feel good. Haven't been fired since college when I got caught sleeping on the graveyard shift."

Jack studied the floor mat. "Money is still okay. Harkness gave me a few months' severance when he threw me out." He exhaled through his nose, and slid lower into his high-backed chair, silent. "The market is really slowing down," he eventually continued. "The long-awaited collapse of commercial real estate seems to have arrived. First the 'Rust Belt'. Then the 'Oil Patch' and the 'Sun Belt' and finally here. Firms are cutting back. It could get rough finding a job."

Ian stared up Ocean Avenue. "I could pass on college for a year or so, Dad. Go to work in a couple of months, if it will help out." He made no attempt at eye contact.

Jack sat up straight, reached over and tousled Ian's hair. "Not that bad yet, kid." He flooded with warmth. "There's some hope. The ACRE office in Ontario is still on a roll, and their number two manager just got promoted. Maybe I can get that."

"That's why you're seeing Mr. Grazlyn?" Ian asked.

Jack nodded. "Since he went to Ontario his career has sky-rocketed. He's become a very big hitter in that office. Close to a seven-figure income I hear. So, I'm gonna ask old friend Mike to recommend to Miles Preston that he give serious consideration to Mike's old friend, Jack. Got it?"

"All but one little part. Who's Miles Preston?"

"He's the guy that runs that office, and he'll be the one deciding who and when on the new sales manager. I don't know him; never even met the guy."

"So my part is to play chauffeur, do a polite 'Hello' to Mr. Grazlyn, and disappear out to the beach for ….how long?" Ian asked.

"Oh, Lord, I may have reared an irreverent son, but he is quick." Jack raised his eyes heavenward. "Ten minutes will do." He sat forward abruptly, and pointed. "We're here. Triple garage on the left. Big guy with the black hair hanging in his eyes standing in front. Try not to run him over, okay?"

As Ian pulled into the shade of the building, Mike Grazlyn

looked up. He was in his mid-thirties, a little over six feet tall and powerfully built even though his waistline had disappeared and a slight paunch was starting to develop. He wore shorts and a T-shirt and had flip-flops on his feet. Mike unleashed a broad, easy smile as Jack opened the door and climbed down.

"Jack, you old sumbitch," Mike said as he walked to the side of the Blazer. "How the hell are ya?"

The two men shook hands. Ian climbed down and came around to join them. "Mike, you remember my son, Ian? Ian, say 'Hello' to Mr. Grazlyn."

Mike directed his big smile toward Ian, "Mr. Grazlyn! Horse-shit. Anyone I have to look up to can call me Mike."

Ian took the extended hand with just a trace of youthful unease. "Thank you, Mike. It's a pleasure to meet you again."

After a few moments of conversation, first about Ian's school, and then about the weather the Santa Anas had brought, Ian excused himself and headed toward the beach.

Jack and Mike moved a few steps into the cool of the garage. "Your boy's growing up," Mike said. "Hell, he's taller than either of us. Good lookin' and well mannered. You should be proud."

"I'll buy into all of it except maybe the well mannered. He can be very willful." Despite his complaint, Jack swelled with pride.

"Consider the source, ol' buddy." Mike pushed the mop of black hair back over his forehead.

"You may have a point," Jack admitted. Then he asked, "What about yours? They must be quite the young ladies by now."

Now it was Mike's turn to beam. "They are. Eight and ten. Both pretty as their momma. Terri, she's the older, pitches a softball high and tight. She's left-handed. Scares hell out of half the damn league."

"Takes after her dad, I see," Jack said, and both men laughed.

There was a moment of stillness before Mike's face broke open into another of his broad smiles. "On the phone, you said I could help you, but you didn't say how. What do you need?"

"I hear you guys in Ontario are without a sales manager." Jack left a little pause.

"And you'd like the job."

Jack couldn't tell if it was a question or a statement. "I'd like to talk about it."

"I sorta thought that would be it. I heard about you and Harkness. What the hell happened?"

"The star—Donaldson," Jack let out a long exhale before he continued. "He represented both sides of a very large office lease. Landlord knew, but the tenant didn't. The tenant thought Donaldson was their guy the whole time. That he was gonna skin the landlord for them. Donaldson said the consent form was coming and left on vacation. By year-end, no consent form," Jack turned both his palms upward. "Harkness wanted to book the income."

"And you wouldn't sign off?" Mike asked.

Jack gave a shrug of his shoulders by way of an answer.

"Well, shit, Jack. How long ago was it you left sales and took over the management of that office?" Mike asked. "Five years?"

"Five," Jack confirmed.

"Five fuckin' years is a long run with that old bird. He'd skin his mother for a hundred dollars. Between your moral compunctions and your thick Irish skull, I'm surprised you made it as long as you did."

"Moral compunctions! Look who's talking," Jack exclaimed. "I'm not the one that spent my formative years having my head pounded by Jesuits."

"When you're trained by Jebbies," Mike responded, "you're trained to make a pretty good moral argument for almost any position you want to stake out. It's a damn helpful skill sometimes. Speaking of help, you probably don't know Miles."

Jack shook his head. "I called him on Friday and introduced myself. I've got an appointment to see him Monday. Will you put in a word for me?"

"Christ. You know I will," Mike answered. "First thing Monday morning." Mike turned to an old refrigerator in the corner. Without looking back, he asked, "Beer?"

"Sure."

Cold air rushed across Jack's cheek as Mike took out two cans and handed one to him. Jack pulled the tab, and took a drink. "What's he like?"

"Less there than meets the eye," Mike answered after chugging half his beer, "but he gets by. You know Miles and our illustrious president came up together as salesmen in New York?"

"I'd heard that," Jack answered. "The word I got was that they're pretty tight."

"Right on," Mike responded. "About a year ago the old boss, guy named Jim Duran—very dynamic—left. Became a developer. The new pres immediately brought his old buddy out from New York."

"Fair-haired boy, eh?"

"He's not so fair-haired anymore." Mike's grin took on a devilish aspect. "Bald as a baby's ass." He laughed heartily.

"Okay, wrong term," Jack conceded with a chuckle. "Maybe it's safer to say he's got pull."

Mike's expression turned serious. "I don't think that's right either."

Jack maintained eye contact but said nothing.

"Miles has fucked up a time or two and his buddy's had to save him." Mike let the sentence trail off and took another swallow.

"Inquiring minds want to know," Jack prodded.

"When he first got here, Miles was in the process of a divorce. A messy one. I think coming west got him away from it. There was a little dalliance one night in his office with our young, impressionable, and very stacked receptionist. Later, she made problems for him. Used to happen all the time. Damn shame the company doesn't tolerate it anymore." Mike's eyes twinkled mischievously. He took a final pull on his beer, crumpled the can and tossed it into a nearby plastic trash can. "I miss the sound they used to make rattling into the old galvanized ones."

"Yeah, satisfying. Manly sound. So what the hell happened?"

"Our illustrious president bailed his ass out. The receptionist is gone, but it cost Miles most of his 'ol' buddy' chits." Mike placed his back against a support post and rubbed back and forth scratching. "Want another beer?"

Jack shook his head. "How are things now?"

"Miles could use some help. He's got problems that are bigger than he is."

"Like what?" Jack asked.

Just then, Ian's blond head appeared around the corner of the house. "Is it safe to come back yet, or should I go body surfing?"

Mike smiled and beckoned, and the tall, thin teenager unwrapped his body from the side of the house and joined them. Looking into the garage, Ian faced toward an enormous stuffed marlin hanging across the width of all three stalls. "Mr. Grazlyn... Mike, did you catch that?"

Mike and Jack turned. Mike's face took on the same expression of pleased pride it had when he'd spoken of his daughter's pitching arm.

"Yeah, Ian, I did," he said as he pushed the hair out of his eyes. "I caught it two years ago off the Bay of Islands in New Zealand. According to Boone & Crockett, it's the second largest black marlin ever taken out of those waters."

Jack looked perplexed. "Why hang something that magnificent in the garage? Surely there's an empty wall for it upstairs."

"There is," Mike answered, "but, it's too big to go up the stairs. It won't go around the corner at the landing—too long. The only way to get it upstairs is to cut a hole in the roof, and Alice won't have the noise and the dust. So here he stays."

Ian frowned. "Why not just cut the bill off and glue it back once it's upstairs?"

Mike turned slowly to look directly at Ian and spoke with

utmost seriousness. "This was a magnificent, powerful beast with the heart of a hero. I fought him for close to two hours. I got him to the boat three times and each time he ran again, stripping the line off that big Daiwa reel until it sang. The crew had to pour buckets of water on it to keep it from overheating and seizing up. I had every advantage of equipment and boat, and he still almost beat me. He was…is…courageous and wonderful. I bested him and it cost him his life. I killed him, but I'll be damned if I'll defile or desecrate his carcass."

* * *

"Dad, what was all that about with the fish?" Ian negotiated the corner onto Marine Avenue by sliding between a slightly out of control skateboarder and a bicyclist with a surfboard under his arm.

"Mike is a man of principles, it appears."

"Principles? Like don't defile any of your dead enemies. Especially, if they're fish. Some principle. Does the driver's exam include a slalom course?" Ian braked to allow a trailing six-year-old to cross in pursuit of his jaywalking parents.

"No slalom as far as I know, but they might add one for residents of the South Bay who plan to drive within a half mile of the beach on weekends." Jack's index finger pushed on the bridge of his sunglasses moving them higher on his nose. "The fish isn't the point. You understand that, don't you?"

"If the fish isn't the point, what is?"

Jack looked out the windshield at the hoard of sun worshippers walking, pedaling and pushing toward the beach. "Virtue," Jack said.

"You're gonna have to use a few more words if you expect me to get this."

"Okay," Jack turned until he faced his son's profile. "If you want the world to be a better place, who do you have to struggle with?" Jack paused, staring at Ian to see what reaction his words were having.

"Not some lame-o fish," Ian's tone had an edge.

"We agree on that," Jack placated. "Not the lame-o fish. But who?"

"I don't know. The bad guys?"

"Who's that, Ian?" Jack tried to mask his sharp focus with a soft voice.

Ian said nothing, but appeared to concentrate on his driving. After he stopped at the light at Manhattan Beach Blvd., he looked over at his father. "Jaywalkers."

Jack hid behind his glasses and didn't speak.

Ian finally continued, "Add corrupt politicians, corporate crooks and drug runners." He looked at his father with a noncommittal expression.

"Speaking of politicians," Jack spoke with a start and suddenly stuck his head out of the window. "Parker! Parker Starling!" he shouted at a middle-aged man in baggy shorts and a Hawaiian shirt rolling through the crosswalk in front of them.

The man shifted his weight to the rear of the skateboard he was riding and stopped by dragging its back along the asphalt. He stood in the crosswalk; his left foot raised high on the front of the skateboard, and turned his head toward the shout. As his eyes panned toward Jack, he smiled widely, "Jack, long time," and then his expression became mockingly stern. "What are you grinning at?"

"Not every day you see a senator's aid on a skateboard," Jack answered.

"Pressing the flesh, beach style."

The light turned green. A car honked its annoyance at the delay.

Jack's friend lowered the front of the board back to the ground, pushed once and rolled through the crosswalk, up the curb cut and onto the sidewalk. "Call me," he shouted over his shoulder. "Here or in Sacramento."

Jack waved as Parker disappeared into the crowd, and then pulled his head back inside the car.

Ian started through the intersection. "Who was that?" he asked.

"Old friend from college. He's the executive aide to our state senator."

"Oh."

They were silent for a block, and then Jack said, "You've left someone out."

Ian glanced over his shoulder. "We're still on bad guys?"

Jack nodded.

"Dad, I've left half the world out. There's not time enough to complete that list."

"All right, you've left out the most important person."

Ian abruptly pulled over to the curb and stopped. After he'd put the Blazer into park he removed his sunglasses and with slow deliberation placed them on the dash and turned to focus entirely on his father. "Okay, who?"

"Yourself."

"Huh?"

Jack squared his hips in the seat to face Ian and then he too removed his sunglasses. "It's a simple question, Ian. Is the struggle for a better world between a man and the evil outside him or is it between him and his own nature?"

The two continued to look at each other for a moment. Ian disengaged, put his sunglasses back on and pulled away from the curb and into the stream of traffic. They remained silent as they drove back up the series of dunes toward Pacific Coast Highway. As they sat at the light waiting to cross, Ian turned to look at his father. "So Mike doesn't weak out and indulge himself. He holds to his principle even if it means he can't have what he wants. It's a character thing?"

Jack smiled, and without raising his head from the high seat back, looked over his left shoulder at his son, and said, "Yeah, Ian. It's a character thing."

CHAPTER 4

Interview

AS JACK wheeled the Blazer into the Starbucks lot he couldn't help but notice the white Lexus with the car-phone antenna on the back window parked in the handicapped spot by the front door. The vanity plates read TOP DOG. His handicap isn't a lack of ego, Jack thought, as a wry grin turned up the corners of his lips.

He parked and walked in to get the last thing he needed before the interview—a double espresso. The line consisted of only one woman. She was tall and wearing a stunning grey worsted suit tailored to emphasize her long legs. The three-inch heels added to the overall effect of sexy elegance. But the most noticeable thing about her was the phone. She had one of those new Motorola car-phones you could unplug from the cradle and carry with you.

"Damn it, John. I don't give a shit what he wants. He gives us the three dollars a foot in tenant-improvements or we take our deal somewhere else. Got it?" she barked into the phone, and then without missing a beat said to the counterman. "If you didn't use non-fat in that latte you can make it over."

"Si, señora," came the subdued response. "We do it again."

"You tell him that, John. And tell him I'm tired of screwing with this. We have a deal by this afternoon or we're outta there and on down the road."

She said no more, but pulled the phone down from her ear

and stuffed it in the large black-leather bag that hung over her shoulder.

Forceful, Jack thought.

The woman in front pulled a wallet from the bag. "Come on," she demanded.

The counterman returned with the corrected coffee.

"Apologies for the delay, Señora."

She grabbed the cup from the counter and swung around with such speed that the cup in her extended hand slammed into Jack's arm. A stream of rich brown-colored liquid jumped out of the cup and rushed through the air toward him. Jack instinctively leaped to one side. He felt the impact as his knee slammed into the edge of a chair and then grabbed at its back as he struggled to keep his feet.

The stream of coffee landed on the floor and splattered, narrowly missing him. Jack heard the slow sharp tap of high heels on the tile floor as they walked away.

He looked up to see the tall woman in the grey suit open the door and then turn to speak again to the counterman. She pointed to the spilt coffee. "You better mop that up before someone slips on it and hurts themselves," she instructed. She turned again walked to the white Lexus, slid in, turned it on and peeled out.

What a bitch, Jack thought.

*   *   *

Jack pulled into the parking lot of the American Corporate Real Estate Ontario office five minutes early for his 11:00 A.M. appointment with Miles Preston. He finished the last sip of his espresso as he parked. Before he got out Jack adjusted the mirror and checked his appearance one last time. He had on his "performance suit." It was a glen plaid, double-breasted Southwick. White pima cotton, spread collar, well-starched shirt, black club tie with purple pheasant pattern, and black Ferragamo wing tips completed the ensemble. The thought that they're still well shined instead of coffee stained thanks only to his quick reflexes brought a small smile.

Jack combed his thinning brown hair straight back. Though forty-five, his blue eyes were crystal clear and the skin of his face still taut—reflections of his discipline in diet and exercise.

He'd joined in the dissipation of the 'seventies, but had woken up at thirty-five divorced, fat and broke. Ten years later he looked the sober, middle-aged citizen he now was and hoped it would project in the coming interview.

He was as prepared as he could get, and stepped out of the car and walked across the lot. Parked right beside the front door was a white Lexus. TOP DOG. Why am I not surprised, he thought as he walked in.

"Miles Preston is expecting me," he said to the receptionist. "I'm Jack Kendrick."

As he waited, Jack surveyed the office that opened up behind the switchboard. For the most part it looked like any other commercial real estate office—one large room separated by chest-high partitions, a bullpen. Two sides were bordered by private offices and conference rooms, and the other two with cubicles for word processors.

What was different about this bullpen was its energy. It was alive, filled with constant background noise from chattering computer keyboards and ringing telephones. The foreground noise was a chorus of forty or so commercial brokers plying their trade, selling over the phone. Three or four of them stood with telephone handsets glued to their ears.

The steady thump of a big Xerox photocopier pounded through the back wall, and the switchboard operator's voice periodically covered all other noises with the polite insistence of a page. Files, papers and brochures leaked out of some of the cubes and into the aisle ways. In others, similar papers grew into precarious towers leaning out over the partitions. Clumps of green potted plants were regularly spaced around the room. Jack thought this attempt at gentility seemed bizarrely out of place.

He could see that many of the brokers had decorated the

counter space and walls of their cubes with photos, plaques and framed newspaper clippings commemorating past accomplishments.

"So what do you think of it?" a voice behind him asked.

Jack turned to face the man he knew must be Miles Preston. Standing before him was the image of patrician gentility. Preston was about six feet tall and held himself rigidly erect. His most distinguishing feature was his smoothly bald head, its crown ringed by a thick fringe of silver hair. He wore it like a victory laurel. His face had the deep tan of a tennis player. The dark tone of his skin gave the blue of his eyes a penetrating quality, commanding notice.

"Looks different than other brokerage offices, doesn't it?" Miles inclined his shiny pate toward the bullpen.

"Hello, Miles," he said, extending his hand. "Jack Kendrick. Pleased to meet you."

"Yes, it does, but it's a lot busier than most of them. That floor," Jack pointed across the reception desk, "looks exciting."

"It's very exciting," Miles said. "This is the largest volume office in the company. Come on back to my office, and let's talk about it." Miles gestured across the room to the corner office.

As he crossed the room, Jack nodded to several of the brokers he knew, and couldn't help wondering if they had figured out, or heard from Mike Grazlyn, why he was here. From a cube in the back of the room, he saw Mike smiling at him. When their eyes met, they nodded imperceptibly but knowingly at each other. It made Jack feel more comfortable.

He also saw the tall woman who'd almost knocked him over at Starbucks. She was standing at a cube across from Mike. Her jacket was off. The pearl necklace she wore was long enough to hang down the front of her blouse and cause its white silk to outline and emphasize her full breasts. She had swept her light-brown, shoulder length hair off one side of her face with the phone that was jammed into her ear. She had large brown eyes, but the rest of her face was long and angular. Long thin nose. Cold, thin, almost pinched lips. It was a face more compelling than attractive. The bitch is a bit of a babe, Jack thought.

Miles' voice brought him back from his appraisal. "You know Liz?" he asked.

"We haven't been introduced, but I couldn't help noticing her. Generally, it's men who stand during phone conversations."

"Liz Peterson is unique in a lot of ways. A little aggression on the phone is the least of them. Here we are," Miles said as they entered the corner office, and motioned Jack to the couch before picking up the phone and giving the switchboard instructions to hold his calls. Then Miles sat in the large leather wing chair across from Jack.

Miles started the interview with background questions, the sort men use to find common ground and judge the life experience and character of others they may need to rely on.

School?—Football powerhouse.

Degree?—Business.

Service?—Marine Corps.

Married?—Several times.

Children?—One son. Recently moved in after years with his mother.

Golf?—High eighties.

And then came the questions that would bring the interview into closer focus

Early career?—Sales and sales management in business machines.

Reason for change?—To get into "bigger ticket" items. Read that, "more money."

Time in commercial real estate?—Fifteen years.

And finally the question they'd been approaching slowly for half an hour.

"Why did you leave Southern California Commercial Properties, Jack?"

"Do you know Ira Harkness?" Jack slid into the answer he'd

prepared for this moment. "He's the President of So Cal Commercial."

"Never met him. Only know his name," Miles answered.

"He's run it for a long time and has a stable of favorite salesmen. They're generally the big producers, the old lions." Jack heard himself speaking as though he was eavesdropping on his own conversation. It was the hearing of a salesman trained to listen and self-correct, both actor and director at once. Was it working? Was Miles accepting his side of the story? "I had a run-in with one of them. He wanted a deal booked. Wanted to receive his check. He'd represented both parties to a lease, but didn't have the tenant's consent. I insisted he have it before we booked the deal and distributed the revenue. Harkness sided with the salesman."

Preston's expression gave away none of his thoughts. He sat quietly with the tips of his fingers pressed together, and stared at Jack, poker-faced. This was it. If Preston judged his action as overzealous or rigidly legalistic, Jack had no chance at this job.

"And you wouldn't back down?" Preston asked.

"No." Jack had an impulse to explain, but controlled it.

"Did you know Harkness was going to fire you if you didn't?" Miles continued.

"Yes, I saw it coming to that."

"And you wouldn't back down?"

"No."

Miles' face still contained no hint of expression. He leaned forward, "Why not?"

"Miles, I'm not certain I can give you a simple answer," Jack said after a moment's reflection. "Stubborn? Maybe, but I don't think so. Right and wrong? Maybe, but I'm sure not without my own sins. Close as I can come is that it was an issue of control."

"Control?"

"Real estate is very entrepreneurial. It attracts very independent sorts. You'd agree with that?" Jack asked.

"Go on," Miles commanded.

"And we don't even pay them. They get half of what they bring in. Makes it damn tough to control them." Jack stopped speaking and waited for agreement.

He got a nod from Miles, no more.

"So how do we control them?" Jack waited for an answer.

"It's your story," Miles said. "You tell me."

"A little moral authority, and a lot of force of will. That's how." Jack paused. "If I let Harkness undermine my authority, the job would have become impossible anyhow."

Miles' face continued to show no expression. "Would you do it again, Jack?" he asked. "Before you answer, let me give you my take on reality. I'm the Senior Operating Officer of what is arguably the largest commercial real estate operation in LA. To the best of my knowledge, I'm the only person in town interviewing for a Sales Manager. And my take is that it will be a long while before there are any other jobs. Revenues are dropping everywhere. Every brokerage operation in town is starting to reduce payroll. High-priced payroll first. I seriously considered not filling this vacancy, but the place is just too big for me to manage it by myself. You don't get this job...." Miles left the sentence unfinished. "That's my take on reality. Now let me ask you, would you do it again?"

Now it was Jack who leaned forward. He made certain he had direct eye contact with Preston before answering. "Yeah, Miles, I'd do it again." And then he leaned back and waited.

Miles stood and walked over to his desk. He turned the pages of his day planner, looked back at Jack and asked, "You like the ponies?"

CHAPTER 5

"And They're Off"

THE GROUND trembled under Jack's feet. He placed a hand on the steel railing. It wasn't his imagination. The railing was vibrating. Then he heard the screams. The whole crowd screamed. And loudest of all was his own voice. Screaming over the din. Hunks of earth flew into the air, and Jack found he had lost all self-control. He jumped up and down, shouting, "Run! Run, God damn it! You got it. Come on. Run!"

And then the horses were past. A final shout of jubilation from the hundreds in the crowd who rode the winner followed by a collective groan of disappointment from the thousands who didn't, and it was over.

"Exciting, isn't it?" Miles asked. "I always enjoy a race more when I come down here by the rail. Well, thirty minutes to the next post. Shall we go back up to the Turf Club and order lunch?" Miles nodded his bald head to a gate in the grandstands above them.

"Wow! I had forgotten what a thrill this is." Jack found himself still shaking with a belly full of adrenaline, and nothing to do with it. "I had a roommate in college who tried to make his tuition at the racetrack. I went with him a few times, but that's been years. What a rush."

They followed the crowd away from the rail and through the litter of discarded betting slips up the grandstands. Miles led the way to the turnstile. Each placed his hand, palm down, under an

39

ultraviolet lamp, showing the attendant the stamps that allowed them access to the covered area of grandstand that was the Turf Club. The rows were much wider here—wide enough to permit small tables instead of the bleacher seats found in the public portion of the grandstand. A white linen cloth, stemware, silver plate and a small bud vase festooned each of them. A narrow aisle passed behind the tables. A steel railing separated the diners in the aisle above from the passersby below.

Miles headed for a reserved table, two rows up and about halfway across. As they approached, a tuxedoed waiter said, "Good afternoon, Mr. Preston. It's nice to have you with us today."

Miles acknowledged the greeting and before he sat in the offered chair, reached into his jacket pocket and produced a betting slip, which he handed to the waiter. "While we look at the menu, would you cash this for me?" And then nodding at Jack, "He can cash your winnings too."

Jack didn't have a winning ticket and said so. After Miles ordered a sherry and Jack a mineral water, the waiter left to collect Miles' winnings and their drink orders. Both men were silent for a moment, and Jack found himself relishing the beauty of the place.

Directly in front of them was the legendary Santa Anita track. The infield was a park, half full of picnicking race fans. But the truly extraordinary part was the backdrop. The San Gabriel Mountains. So close they appeared to be just beyond the parking lot. Straight up, rugged and snow-capped. Jack could practically see the streams of snow melt running off. Here it was eighty degrees and sunny, but the snow-covered mountains seemed almost close enough to touch.

Miles studied the view. "Sure beats Northeasters coming off the Atlantic. It's one of the reasons I like it here."

Jack waited as Miles eased the conversation toward the business they came to conduct.

"Jack, on Monday I told you that our office was the largest branch in the company," Miles said with some pride. "And we're not just bigger, we're different. We operate with our own unique system. Most offices have thirty or forty brokers out there doing their own thing, as the expression goes. In ours, most of the brokers work together. Part of a team you might say. Each one has a role to play. Some of those roles are big ones, and some are small. In fact, you might say we've got a star system. A couple of stars and a lot of supporting cast."

"Are the bit players willing to stay in smaller roles?" Jack asked. "Brokers are attracted to this business by the chance to star."

Before Miles could respond the waiter returned with their drinks. "Mr. Preston, your Dry Sack. And, sir," with a nod to Jack, "your mineral water." And then handing Miles an envelope, he said, "Your wager, Mr. Preston, Moon Mist to place. Are you ready to order, gentlemen?"

"We really haven't looked," Miles responded and then looked at Jack. "But if you'll allow me, Jack, I'd suggest the petrale. If you like fish, it's excellent. That and perhaps a Caesar salad."

"Sounds fine. Petrale and Caesar it is. And maybe a glass of wine." Jack addressed the waiter. "Do you have any whites besides Chardonnay?"

"Yes, sir. A nice Sauvignon Blanc. Frog's Leap from last year."

"That will be fine. Miles, care to join me?"

The orders were taken, and the waiter left. Jack asked, "Miles, you had Moon Mist to place. Are you always so cautious?"

"Cautious?"

"Moon Mist was the favorite," Jack explained. "Went off at about eight to five. And you took a place bet. Betting favorites to come in second is pretty cautious."

"I'll leave risky bets to other men—younger men. At this stage in life, I want to cash in all my bets." Miles paused. "You asked about controlling the ambitions of the bit players? Those bit players are making more in our shop than the stars in some others. Also, it helps to understand how it all came to be." Miles sipped the last of his sherry and eased further into his chair.

"Ten years ago, Liz Peterson came to the company as a twenty-one-year-old straight out of college. She was assigned to Paul Jensen for a year's training—a runnership. At the end of that year, Paul made what was arguably the most brilliant move of his career. He invited Liz to join him as a fifty-fifty partner. She was twenty-two years old, still wet behind the ears, never made a deal, and full partner to a journeyman producer."

Jack sat forward, listening intently. Miles went on.

"Paul was right. The partnership worked brilliantly and within a year he went from being a journeyman producer to a star. He and Liz constantly had runners. And when their training was complete, those runners, if they were any good, were invited to remain as commission participants on specific projects. Of course, the new guys did all of the work and gave two-thirds of the income to Paul and Liz. But as new salespeople they benefited by being invited into large, prestigious and revenue producing projects. It was better than starting with nothing, and very few of their trainees said no to the offer.

"Eventually there were at least a dozen commission sales people in one corner of the office, all basically working for Paul and Liz. That group became like a black hole. Everything that came near their portion of the universe was sucked in. They did all of the business; they were in command of the market.

"But like many good combinations, it had a fatal flaw."

"Mr. Preston, may I move your Racing Form?" the waiter asked.

"Oh, of course. Time for us to stop talking business anyhow. They've sounded parade to post. We've got just enough time to check the second race entries. Any minute now, they'll come out the tunnel." Miles pointed up the track behind Jack. "You can borrow my binoculars if you'd like a closer look."

"No thanks, Miles. I don't know enough to look that close. If one of them is prancing, got its tail held high and isn't grey it will probably do for me. And I can tell all of that without the glasses."

The waiter finished serving their meal. "Will there be anything else, gentlemen?"

"Yes," Miles responded. "Would you stop by after the parade and place a bet for us?"

The waiter agreed and left. "So, no grey horses for you, eh, Jack? And no information from the Racing Form either?" Miles asked.

"On the contrary, I'd like to borrow yours if I may. The Number Five horse prancing along. The big strawberry roan with its nose stuck in the neck of its lead pony. What's its speed rating?"

"It's named 'Good Job'. The tote board is showing it currently at eight to one. Bit of a long shot."

Jack accepted the paper Miles passed across the table. After minutes' reflection, he sat it down, picked up his fork and cut off a bite of the sole on his plate. "You're right, Miles. Excellent fish. Thanks for the suggestion. See anything you like in the second race?"

"Top Spin strikes my fancy. I think I'll parlay my winnings from the first race."

"On a place bet?" Jack asked.

Miles didn't answer and continued with his lunch. The waiter came back as he'd promised and both men gave him their selections and money.

After he left Jack said, "What was the fatal flaw?"

Miles took a sip of his wine and then dipped the glass toward Jack in a small toast. "Good selection. I'll remember." And then after a moment of reflection, continued. "The essence of the problem was age. Liz is in her early thirties and Paul is in his early fifties. They want different things. Liz wants control of everything. She is the spider woman. She wants the net ever bigger. Paul wants to spend less time building the net and more time enjoying what's already been collected. He wants the ranch in New Mexico and tuna trophy mounts. What he doesn't want is to spend all of his time making money."

"That shouldn't be difficult," Jack commented. "Senior partners bow out all the time. Liz takes more control; Paul takes less money. Simple."

"Money." Miles used his fork to gesture toward Jack. "You named the problem. Paul doesn't want to give any up. Liz tried to tell Paul that there had to be adjustments. He had to give up some of his share or he had to come back to work.

"But Paul didn't see it that way. By him, he'd put the whole damn thing together. He'd made Liz and all those young brokers rich and now they could feed him for awhile. Liz and the others didn't see it that way. The whole thing finally fell apart.

"When it did, most of those young brokers saw Liz as the future. They stuck with her. Paul was seen as the past and had very few allies around the office. He asked me to hire his son and I did. I couldn't say no, but Brent was not someone I'd normally hire. He's aggressive enough and has a good work ethic, but he's not his dad. Brent's not a salesman. That's obvious to everyone around him. Everyone except his father.

"The split-up has also had the effect of making our office combative. Paul and Liz would rather see each other lose a deal than make one. If, as the old bromide says, the only thing sweeter than making a deal is seeing a friend blow one, our office has become a very sweet place indeed. And it's costing us business."

"The horses are at the starting gate," a baritone voice intoned over the public address system.

"Too late to get down to the rail," Miles said as he picked up the binoculars. "We'll watch from here."

The starting bell rang loudly, but just before it sounded Jack saw the gates fly open and the horses break through. The distance from his seat to the starting gate, positioned on the far side of the track, was great enough that the sight came ahead of the sound.

All eight horses broke together and for the first hundred yards they hurtled down the track and swept to the left to hug close to the rail. A small black in pink and purple silks surged to the front and opened up three lengths on the pack. As they raced along the backstretch in a ballet of speed and power, three horses dropped out of the pack and fell off the pace. 'Good Job,' 'Top Spin' and two other horses matched strides and remained three lengths in back of the black as they ran down the backstretch and rounded the far turn. As they entered the clubhouse turn, the pack started to close the lead. That they'd pass the black became certain. The only question was how. One of the pack tried to squeeze by on the inside but the black hung tenaciously to the rail as they rounded the turn. The inside horse was stuck.

The other three swung by on the outside and into the final straightaway. The crowd rose to its feet, trying, by force of will, to pull one of the three ahead of the others. Miles' 'Top Spin' had been forced to swing wider than the other two when passing the black, and couldn't seem to make up the extra ground he'd been forced to cover.

Jack's 'Good Job' was running stride for stride with a big grey in white silks. Each extending almost flat and then rising up before stretching again. The winner would be whichever was stretched forward when they reached the wire.

It was the grey.

Miles and Jack looked away from the tape and toward each other. Neither man was smiling.

"You have that strawberry roan to win?" Miles asked.

Jack reached into his pocket, took out his betting slip, and slowly ripped it in half. "And you had the favorite to place again?" he asked in return.

Miles' face cracked into a sardonic smile, and he repeated Jack's gesture. "You picked the better horse, but you still lost." And then he added, "If you'd have exercised a bit of my caution, you'd have won."

"True," Jack responded. "It's also true that it's hard to win enough to pay for lunch betting favorites to come second. You'd do better by taking a risk now and then."

"Where I really need help is at the office not the track." Miles was suddenly all business. "You think you can help me there, tell me how you'd do it."

Jack took his time. "The solution is simple," he finally said. "Not easy, but simple. Slap one of them. Real hard! Paul, Liz and their friends have to understand management won't tolerate their feud. The success of the office is more important."

Miles didn't change his expression. His body lay deep in the chair, as though bereft of starch and energy. For a moment he remained silent. Finally, he exhaled deeply, took a small breath, and pulled himself forward.

"Jack, at ACRE a manager is viewed as a hundred-thousand-dollar expense item on the company books. Paul may be the past but he's still a huge producer. He and Liz are each viewed by senior management as about a two-million-dollar income item. It could be very dangerous for any manager to seriously upset either one. Neither of them would have the slightest hesitation about going over your head or mine, and my superiors would not look with favor on any action viewed as a threat to the revenue generated by their number one office."

Miles gazed at the mountains for a moment, and then continued. "I'm less than ten years from retirement, and have big alimony and mortgage payments. I have no intention of getting crushed between those two. You want the job, it's yours."

*   *   *

Lorna reached across the table and clinked her glass against Jack's. "To my hero who just slayed another dragon."

"It's nice to be appreciated." The warmth Jack felt toward her was evident in his tone. "But I'm not sure this dragon won't end up eating me."

"Sweetie, don't worry so very much. Celebrate a little. Six weeks ago we were a family with mortgage payments, college tuition starting soon, no predictable income after the three months severance from So Cal Commercial ran out, and very bleak job prospects. Look what you pulled off. About the only job in town, and you landed it. That means our finances are okay again, and your bride has all that leftover severance pay to blow. Now stop worrying and be my hero, at least for tonight."

Jack just smiled and looked across the table at the woman he had married. She had high cheekbones, a straight strong nose, full lips and still no wrinkles. Well, maybe one forming at the corner of each eye, but the light would have to be a lot harsher than this to see them. Her dark brown hair had just enough red in it to look auburn in the candlelight, and her eyes were exactly the same color. Jack thought, you did good for a middle-aged guy.

"Okay, honey. That's an offer with far too much promise to refuse. Tonight, I'll be your hero."

Now Lorna smiled, and said with coquettish mimicry. "Promise? Did I make any promise?"

She may have expected a smile from Jack at her flirtation, but he looked past her and out the restaurant window at King Harbor. There was no moon, but the starlight and the lights on the pier gave just enough illumination to outline the masts slowly swaying as the boats beneath gently rocked with the incoming tide.

"Sweetie?" Lorna's smile was gone. "You look so serious. What's wrong?"

"Hon, I'm sure it will be fine. But..." Jack paused, "if this thing doesn't work out with ACRE, there might not be another severance package. We might need that money yet."

"You're really worried about it, honey?" Lorna seemed, for the first time, to really register his fear.

"Miles Preston has hired me to do something that he doesn't have the guts to do. Or maybe he's too smart to do."

She said nothing, and he focused on the swaying masts for a moment. "It all seemed so easy when I told Harkness 'no.' At the time, I didn't even think about it. It was the right thing to do, and I did it. But now Lorna, I'm not so sure."

CHAPTER 6

Cattle Baron

THE V–12 Mercedes crested the cliff above Newport Harbor just in time for Paul Jensen to witness the sun burst over the horizon. Its eruption was so forceful that Paul shut off the Zig Ziglar tape for a moment and stared. As he snapped Ziglar's "Secrets of Closing the Sale" back on he thought, the one good thing that has come of Liz breaking up our partnership is that I don't have to listen to the bitch complain about my motivational tapes.

Cruising east along an almost deserted Newport Blvd., toward the San Diego Freeway, Paul couldn't concentrate on Ziglar's message of self-determination. He was still captured by the beauty of the sunrise. But after a few moments of observation, he concluded it wasn't as pretty as watching a New Mexico sunrise where the golden light bathed the Sangre de Cristo Mountains. First, just before the dawn itself, the snowcapped peaks glowed as though burning with a crimson flame, and then the sun rose over the eastern plain, and the light flowed down the slopes and spread over the dew-covered grass below. Eight sections of that grass, over 5,000 acres, were his—Rancho Conquistador.

Paul pulled his sunglasses from the visor and slid them on. Why the hell was he still doing this? And why the hell had that woman put him in the spot where he had to? God damn it, he thought, I made that girl. She'd be running in the middle of the pack, living in Irvine if I hadn't carried her back then. Who the hell cares if I did it for the wrong reason? Who the hell could have known we'd be this good together? And then the corners of his mouth pulled up in a small grin. But she did have great tits. What man wouldn't have wanted her? Thrown together every day for a year. Her, fresh and young. But not so naïve. Oh, he'd thought she was. He'd thought that adulation was real, "Oh, Paul you are so good. How did you figure him out? Stop staring at me. Those green eyes of yours make me weak when you look at me like that." What horseshit. Oh, she let me rub them every now and again, but there was always some excuse. And how was it she'd finally put it, "If we're partners, honey, we'll share everything. Everything. I promise." God's balls, how did anyone that young get so manipulative.

And what the hell was he supposed to do when she didn't. Everybody assumed he was fucking her. Was he supposed to dump the partnership and have everyone laugh? "Girl too much for you, Paul?" "Hey, Paul, couldn't keep up with her?" And damn near before he could decide the money started rolling in. His contacts; her tenacity and energy. Better than he could ever have guessed. He'd become the single most successful salesman in the largest commercial real estate firm in California.

That success had bought him his ranch, and if he had just one more seven-figure year, he'd have that puppy mortgage-free. The ranch house, the barns, fences and equipment were in top shape. If the mortgage were retired he'd be running a five hundred-unit cow-calf operation without debt and a little cash flow. A smooth ride all the way to the grave. But he needed that "one more year," and without it he was stuck. But was he really stuck because of the money, or was it Brent?

Paul still wondered if it had been right to bring his son into the business. Maybe Brent would have been better off if he still worked as a ski instructor at Mammoth or maybe at the ranch? Well, it didn't much matter now. Brent was here; they were partners and the market was a pile of shit. If Paul didn't find the pony under that pile of shit pretty quick, he might never get the debt removed from the ranch. Lord knows his cattle operation didn't make enough to pay the mortgage. Like his daddy had said, "Raising cattle is the most enjoyable way I know to go broke."

And if he didn't get out, he was going to be stuck in a business in which he was losing his grip. Once, he'd known everyone and been known by them. Known and feared just a little. But now everyone was gone or going. All the developers were being taken down by the market and their lenders. The business was being taken over by a bunch of institutional types. Guys with MBAs who didn't know shit about real estate and couldn't make a decision without six spreadsheets, four studies, umpteen computer analyses and committee approval were taking over the business.

Well, all those institutional assholes could take all that paper, make papier-mâché dildos with it, and go fuck themselves for all he cared. Relationships still counted for more than spreadsheets. Like his relationship with Patch Patterson. Thank God for Patch and the Tuna Club. It was relationship and membership in the Club that got him and Patch on that boat together. Two guys become pretty close after years of chasing up and down the Pacific in search of big fish.

The tuna move up from the south with the warm water which usually gets to LA by July or August. It gets to the tip of Baja before then. And this year El Niño, the Christmas current, was rolling north out of the Antarctic and bringing the warm water two months ahead of schedule. The Tuna Club members jumped at the chance to start the season early. So Paul and Patch and all their other buddies flew to Cabo San Lucas, and took a charter boat to power south for two days. They pulled in tuna 'til their arms gave out, and then powered back. On the traveling days, there was nothing to do but drink beer and tequila, play cards and talk. And they did all of it. A lot of all of it. It was in the drinking and the talking that Patch told.

*   *   *

Paul stood alone in the exact peak of the bow of the eighty-five-foot Angler. He had a hand on each gunnel, with his square jaw thrust forward as though he were the bowsprit. A fine spray rushed up from the surface and washed over his face each time the ship broke into one of the gently rolling swells.

"Thought someone up here might need a beer so I brought a spare."

Paul turned to see Patch Patterson lurching toward him; a long-necked Corona clutched in his extended hand. Patch was a tall, thin man in his mid-fifties, and, when sober, looked like a banker, which he was. Now he looked like a fisherman in the middle of a two-day binge, which he was.

Paul accepted the beer and held it with nothing more than the little finger of his large hand curled around the top of the neck. He wrapped his other arm around Patch's shoulders and pulled him forward so he too could wedge into the bow. "You better grab a hold here, buddy. You're drunk enough to pitch right over, and I'm too drunk to catch ya if ya go."

"Shit," Patch adjusted his hands so he clutched the beer and the gunnel with equal fervor, "thirty years o' ridin' these tubs, ain't gone over yet."

They stood side by side wedged into safety.

"Christ, it's beautiful," Patch broke the silence. "Looks like we could ride this moonbeam to heaven." Patch motioned with his nose toward the luminous highway Angler was following as it ran a course straight toward the moon.

"Beats hell out of workin'," Paul laughed in agreement. "Shit, make about as much here as I would workin' anyhow."

"Poker gods that kind to you?"

"It isn't so much the cards are good, Patch," Paul snorted, "as it is the market sucks."

"You think real estate is bad, you should try bankin'. We're not makin' any development loans, and the ones we've made ain't payin' us back. We're about to foreclose on a huge project."

"Huge!" Paul teased. "How huge?"

"About fifty million dollars huge. That big enough for you, asshole?"

Paul whistled. "Once you get it back, what you figure you can sell it for?"

"We'll take a fuckin' bath. Loose maybe twenty million."

Paul was all seriousness now. "I'll get you a buyer, Patch."

Patch sobered. His eyes cleared as he pulled himself to his full height so Paul had to look up just slightly. "Shit, Paul, I tell you; you bring a buyer; the guy we're about to foreclose on sues us. Unlawful fucking interference with his prospective economic gain, it's called. Like the asshole had any chance of prospective economic gain."

With the longneck trapped between his pinkie and ring finger, Paul tilted the Corona toward his mouth, placed his knuckles under his chin and took a pull. He lowered the bottle. "Patch, I only need one more big deal, and I'm a career. No one is ever gonna' know." He stared directly into the moonlit face of his friend of thirty-years.

Patch turned to face the moonbeam connecting them to the heavens and the sea before them. He tilted his bottle, drained it, and then threw it far out into the ocean before he turned to face Paul. "It's Cunningham," he said as he returned his friend's stare. "We're going to foreclose on the Cunningham project."

Paul inhaled sharply, "Holy shit, Cunningham." He said nothing more, but put his arm around Patch's shoulders and the two men stood silently facing the highway to heaven.

CHAPTER 7

Double Dealing

"LIZ PETERSON. Oscar Cornblatt holding for Liz Peterson." The receptionist announcement carried over the general din of the office.

Liz dropped her call and picked up immediately. "Cornie, I was thinking about you this morning. You said Vance Electronics would be ready to move the beginning of June. It's the beginning of June. You coming out soon?"

"Honey, you available tomorrow to show me around that desolate patch of ground you call The Inland Empire?" Before she could answer Cornblatt added, "I mean, girl, what PR man came up with that boondoggle of a name? It's like Lief Erickson naming that piece of ice in the North Atlantic, Greenland. Empire, my ass. Inland Desert is more like it."

"Cornie, you always bitch. It's Southern California's distribution center. All the freeways, rail lines and even an international airport come together here. Who cares if it's ugly? And of course I'm available. When are you arriving? I'll meet your plane."

"As usual, darling, you're right. Maybe, it's ugly, but I don't care. And I'm on my way now. I'll get in this evening, and get myself on over to the Hilton. How about breakfast at the hotel, and then we'll do the grand tour of your Empire."

"I've got a better idea," Liz responded. "How about I meet

your plane, and chauffeur you over to the hotel? After you get unpacked, we can have dinner together and talk about the market. Then tomorrow's tour will be a bit easier. When's your flight arriving?"

"Six-twenty. It's United from JFK. I'd enjoy the pleasure of your company, particularly if you bring along one of those adorable young men you always seem to be training."

Liz laughed. "Sorry, Cornie, it's just me. My last runner is now a full commission guy and on his own. They haven't found me a new one yet. But..." Liz left anticipation in the unfinished comment.

She thumbed through her Vance file, then asked, "Have you looked at the list of available buildings and brochures I sent?"

"Of course I looked, sweetheart. What do you think of me? And I must say, we've got more choices than I expected."

"Rough times for the developers," Liz explained. "They built a lot of big warehouses on spec just before the whole economy crashed. No one's buying. A couple of the developers are in real trouble. Your timing couldn't be better. We'll make a great deal."

She retrieved a brochure. "Did you notice one built by a guy named Max Boswell? One hell of a building, Cornie. And he's a guy we can skin."

"I don't remember," Cornblatt responded. "We'll look tomorrow."

"Take a look at the brochure while you're on the plane," Liz insisted. "It's perfect. See you this evening at six-twenty."

Liz hung up the phone, grabbed her bag and headed for the door.

As she left the switchboard operator caught her eye. "Jack asked me to have you call him when you got off the phone."

"I'll call him from the car, Irene."

*   *   *

"You look comfortable enough."

Jack looked up from the correspondence he was reviewing to

see Miles standing in the doorway. Jack thought again how Miles' fringe of grey hair and ramrod straight posture provided that patrician bearing he used so well.

"Three months should be enough for a guy to get comfortable. Come on in."

"No thanks, I've got some budgeting issues I need to get to while you keep our sales force productive and out of trouble. I just wanted to see if you were free about two o'clock."

"What's up?"

"You're looking for a new runner for Liz. I got a resumé from a kid who's just graduated from Cal Poly Pomona. He called to follow up, and I've got him coming in after lunch. Thought maybe he could see you after he and I finish. Name's Montgomery Pierce."

"How's his resumé look?" Jack asked.

"Not much to tell. Summer jobs and a degree in Finance with an emphasis in Real Estate. Sounds very anxious to learn."

"Send him over when you're through. I've got a call into Liz. She could use him right away, as long as he's willing to work twelve hours a day for a year at slave wages, and doesn't think the big bucks come the day after he's hired."

                              *   *   *

Liz hit the speed dialer on the car phone.

"Jack Kendrick."

"Jack, Irene said you wanted to talk."

"Hi, Liz. You calling from the car?" Jack asked.

"I'm checking out a couple of buildings. You'll be pleased to know that Oscar Cornblatt—he's head of real estate for Vance Electronics—is coming out to look at warehouses. Big warehouses," Liz said. "I'll be representing him. The commission could run as high as three hundred thousand if I can sell him a building where we get a full pop. But sad to tell the best building for the guy is Max Boswell's, and he always lists his buildings with CB Commercial, so I may have to split the commission on the deal."

"That's half of a pretty big loaf," Jack responded. "I called on a much less exciting issue. A new runner. Are you going to be back in the office this afternoon?"

"I'll be back after three. Got a candidate?"

"Maybe," Jack said. "A recent grad from Cal Poly's real estate program. I haven't seen him yet so I don't know if he's good or not. He'll be waiting when you get back. Talk to him and then we'll compare notes."

"Will do. Gotta go. I'm just pulling into Max Boswell's parking lot. Need to make sure he hasn't lost control of those twin turkeys he built. One of them will be perfect for Vance, and I'm sure we can make a deal if his bank hasn't foreclosed yet."

They said quick good-byes as Liz wheeled into one of the vacant spaces in front of Boswell's office. The building was a concrete tilt-up. He had built it as a warehouse, and when the tenant didn't want all of it, Max built some office space for himself at one end. He cut some glass panels into the concrete and pushed several tons of soil in front of the loading dock to make it look like a rolling lawn leading up to office space. To Liz's trained eye it still looked like a converted warehouse.

Liz turned off the ignition, but didn't get out. A deal between Boswell and Vance would generate three hundred thousand dollars in commission. Since Boswell had his building listed, his agent would get half, and ACRE would get half. Liz would get half of what she brought to ACRE—seventy-five thousand dollars. There were buildings she could sell to Vance that were not listed with an agent. No listing agent; no fee split. No fee split, and Liz would double her share to one-hundred-fifty thousand.

But Boswell's building had a special appeal. He was days from foreclosure and vulnerable—very vulnerable. Weak as he'd become, she could force him to take her on as a partner and profit as a principal as well as earning a brokerage commission. It was illegal, of course, and the Real Estate Commissioner would pull her license if she got caught. But, I'm not gonna get caught, she thought.

The receptionist announced her, and Max appeared almost immediately. Liz appraised him as he crossed the room. Max was still trim and had a flat stomach at fifty. She'd guess liposuction rather than sit-ups. He wore linen slacks, Cole Haan loafers with no socks and dress shirt open at the throat. His black hair hung in unruly bangs over his forehead, and his teeth were so white and straight they had to be caps. Right hand firmly extended, he approached her.

"Liz, good of you to stop by," he beamed. "I was especially glad to hear you say it was urgent. Urgent smells like a deal."

Liz remained seated long enough to leave Max momentarily in an awkward position with his hand extended. "Max, thanks for making time. And you're right. Your nose does smell a deal."

"Let's not talk here. Come on back." Max motioned her in front of him to the open door across the office.

As they walked, Liz took in the four vacant desks. Not vacant like someone was away temporarily. Vacant with no clutter or personal mementos on them. It was obvious no one worked there anymore.

Max had furnished his private office with plaid upholstered wing chairs, mahogany-stained wainscoted walls and oriental throw rugs, a British gentlemen's club of a bygone era. A framed eleven by fourteen photograph of four men in knickers and tweed caps holding golf clubs and standing on the tee with a windswept fairway in the background confirmed it.

"St. Andrew's?" Liz asked.

"You've been there?" Boswell's tone was proud. He motioned her to one of the large wingback chairs across from his desk.

"No, just a guess." Liz continued to stand, holding her eyes level with his.

"Happier times," he waxed nostalgic, "when a trip to Scotland to play the old course with friends could be done on a whim."

Liz sat and crossed her knees. She smiled at Boswell. "Well maybe I can help bring those times back. If we do this, it will be a start."

Boswell's face settled into a sober negotiation expression. "What's the deal, Liz?"

"You have twin two-hundred-thousand–square-foot warehouses that you need to unload. I'm here to buy one of them. Actually, I'm here to get an option to buy one of them."

The disappointment showed on Boswell's face. "An option?" he asked rhetorically.

"An option, Max," she sneered, "the right to purchase your building in the future."

"I know what an option is," Max was stern. "It won't work. I need a deal now. I can't take either of the buildings off the market unless the option payment is a lot of money and the option period real short."

"You'll like the term then, Max. One week."

Now Max looked stunned. "One week? You want to option my building for one week?" He held his right hand in his left, and twirled the diamond-encrusted ring on his little finger. "Who's buying the option, and how much will they pay for this one week of control?"

"I told you, Max, I'm the buyer. I'm the one that wants to option it. For a week, and I'll pay you a buck. One buck; one week." She held her face free of all expression.

"You've got a buyer in your pocket, don't you?" Boswell's voice raised a bit.

Liz chose not to respond.

"You expect me to option the building at a price you can increase to your buyer. That's double dealing, sweetie. Playing both ends for a profit. ACRE, the Department of Real Estate and your client wouldn't be real pleased to hear about this." His voice had gotten higher-pitched as well as louder.

"Max, before you get too upset, don't you want to know what option price I'm offering?"

"Okay, Liz, I'll play. What price?"

"Twenty dollars, Max. Twenty dollars per square foot. That's four million dollars."

Max stood. "Twenty dollars? That's what it cost me to build. You and your offer can get the hell out. Now! I'll be on the phone to the President of ACRE and the DRE before you're out of the building," he roared, pointing to the door.

Liz continued to allow herself no expression. She just looked at Boswell, as he stood frozen with his arm extended like a child playing statues. "Max, what is it you're going to say to all these people? That an overextended, middle-age developer who's about to lose everything he owns received an offer to take on a partner who could bring in a buyer and save him and his project?" Liz was silent and just stared at Boswell. "And if you don't, you'll never see the buyer. You won't even know he's in the market. A transaction will be completed and the buyer in another building before you ever have the chance to say, 'Hey, wait, I'll make you a better deal.' And I'll deny everything, and say your accusations are the whining of a bankrupt loser who couldn't make the deal."

Liz fell silent and stared at him with curiosity. Boswell slowly dropped his arm and then just as slowly sat down.

"That's better," Liz said. "Max, I'm not going to rape you. What I want is an option on half the building at cost. We'll be partners. We'll get over five million for the building, and we split the profit. That gives you half a million dollars. I know you're at the spot where you have to give these buildings back to the bank— Inland Empire S & L, isn't it—or start making payments on the construction loan yourself. You don't have the money to make the payments on those notes, and no one's going to loan it to you either. But with a half million dollars, you can make the payments on the second building and keep your operation going for at least six, maybe eight, months. Who knows what can happen in six months? That's a lifetime. The market may be on a roll again. You'll be fine."

Max sat immobile in his overstuffed chair. He was out of fight. She was right, and he knew it.

Liz opened her bag and took out a one-page document. "I took the liberty of having our agreement drawn up." Liz placed it on the desk in front of her and shoved it across to Boswell. "You'll notice the partner isn't Liz Peterson. It's Equity, Inc. You can understand that I'll need this in another name."

Boswell looked at the agreement briefly, took a pen from the desk set in front of him, signed and handed it back to her. Liz folded the document and put it in her bag. She rose to go. "You're taking this the wrong way, Max. An hour ago you didn't know how you were going to survive the end of the month. You've just bought some time—six months, maybe more. Smile, Max."

Max regained some composure. "You plan on this being a commissionable sale?"

Liz feigned surprise, "Max, of course it is. You and your bank have it in the pro forma. There's unfunded money in your loan to cover it. You've listed the property for sale with CB Commercial. Your broker and I need to be paid; we'll share the usual fifty–fifty split."

Liz turned to go. Half way across the room she stopped, opened her bag and took out a dollar bill. Then she turned back to Max. "Oh, I almost forgot," she said holding the bill toward him. "Your option payment."

Max made no move for the money so Liz let go and the bill floated to the floor. "See you tomorrow, partner."

CHAPTER 8

The Candidate

IRENE LED Montgomery Pierce into Jack's office. As she appeared in his doorway, Jack again noticed how striking the bright and energetic young receptionist looked. Dark deep-set eyes gave her a sense of mystery that Jack found impossible to ignore. As the candidate stepped into the room beside her, Jack's first thought was what a handsome couple they make. Like Irene, Montgomery had dark hair, olive skin and finely sculpted features that made him almost as pretty as the girl beside him. But it was his eyes that held Jack. Wide spaced and imparting a sense of vulnerability, they seemed to define him before he even spoke. The image didn't suit a broker in the rough-and-tumble world of commercial real estate, Jack thought.

"Mr. Kendrick, this is Montgomery Pierce." Irene's slight but mellifluous Spanish accent gave the introduction charm. With a small flourish of her hand she directed the young man into the room and then departed.

"Have a seat." Jack stood and stepped around his desk. "Is it Montgomery or do you prefer Monty?"

"Montgomery, sir," he said extending his hand.

"Please, no 'sir' around here. I'm Jack."

Montgomery took a seat in the offered chair as Jack walked back around his desk and sat down. He nodded toward the paper on top of his desk. "Montgomery, about all I get from your resumé is that you've been interested enough in real estate to major in it. Tell me a bit about this interest, and why brokerage. Why not finance, development or any of the other approaches to this business?"

The young man collected himself for a moment before he started. "My interest goes back before college. Some kids want to be attorneys or soldiers. I always wanted to be a commercial broker. So I studied that in school. To prepare."

Jack arched an eyebrow. "You've always wanted to be a commercial broker?" The challenge in his voice was clear.

"Sir?" and Montgomery hesitated.

Jack smiled gently. "Montgomery, we talk to a lot of candidates for runner positions. It's a popular place for graduates to start a career. But I don't think I ever had one tell me brokerage was a childhood dream."

"Well I had a little help."

"Your dad pushed you toward it?" Jack asked.

"No, sir. I never really knew my dad. He didn't come back from Vietnam." Montgomery crossed his knees before continuing. "Mom was the one who pushed me. She always pointed out the brokerage signs, and the names that appeared regularly. I grew up recognizing names like Paul Jensen, Liz Peterson, and Mike Grazlyn." Montgomery uncrossed his knees. "Mom said that fortune waited for me in commercial real estate. I just needed to go get it."

"You're serious." It was Jack's turn to hesitate.

Montgomery said nothing and waited for Jack to ask the next question. "Tell me what you've done to get ready to fulfill this ambition."

And for the next thirty minutes Montgomery explained how his classes, research and summer jobs were all selected to learn more about commercial real estate.

"The summer I turned sixteen, I got a job working as a carpenter's helper with Oltmans' Construction." Montgomery ran a hand through a forest of hair. "I knew they specialized in concrete tilt-up warehouse construction, and I wanted to learn how they were built.

"One day a helicopter circled over the project. We had the dirt pad all formed, but the walls weren't yet tilted."

Jack found himself captivated by Montgomery's story.

"After it circled a few times it dropped to within fifty feet and circled real tight, as though it wanted to land. The crew scampered off the pad, and the helicopter landed. Two guys in white shirts and ties, and an attractive young woman, almost as tall as the men, got out and looked around the site.

"Later, the foreman told me it was Paul Jensen and Liz Peterson showing the building to a client who wanted to buy it." Montgomery peered intently at Jack.

"So?" Jack finally asked.

Montgomery smiled and pushed the hair out of his eyes again. "So right then I knew Mom was right. A fortune did await me in commercial real estate."

Jack twirled a pencil slowly for a moment, and then he focused on the candidate. "Montgomery, you mentioned Liz Peterson earlier. She's looking for a runner. I presume that's of interest to you?"

"Yes," he said, his eyes glowing with anticipation.

"Okay, I expect her back in a bit. Wait in the reception area, and when she comes in, I'll get you two together." Jack rose and handed Montgomery his business card. "Call me after you and Liz have talked."

"Thank you, Jack. I appreciate this," Montgomery said as he extended his hand. "I want this job. I'll do anything it takes to get it."

Jack watched the slim young man cross the office to the waiting area. Instead of taking a seat, he strolled around the room studying the plaques decorating the walls with the intensity of an art student at the MOCA. Jack turned to his phone and punched in Liz's car number.

"Liz, are you on your way back?"

"On my way, and happy to report that Boswell's building is still available. How's the candidate look?"

"I'll be interested in what you have to say about that. He's in the reception area waiting for you," Jack said. "Lord knows he's eager enough."

"I hear a 'but' in there," Liz interrupted.

"I'm not sure he's tough enough for this. There's a vulnerability that bothers me."

"Maybe he's just young, Jack," Liz said.

"Maybe. See what you think."

"What's his name again?"

"Montgomery 'Don't-Call-Me-Monty' Pierce," Jack answered.

"Montgomery. Okay, I'll talk to Montgomery soon. But I may not get back to you until tomorrow. I've got to get over to the airport to pick up Oscar Cornblatt."

*   *   *

Liz eyed the young man studying the 'Salesperson of the Year' plaque. She stopped about four feet behind him. "How many years before you think it will say 'Montgomery Pierce' up there?"

He turned with a start and Liz too was taken aback. Before her was the face of one of the best looking men she'd ever seen. Jack didn't tell me about that.

"You're Liz."

She offered her hand, "And you're Montgomery."

Liz nodded toward the conference room beside them. "Let's step in here and talk. I haven't got long, but we can spend a few minutes together."

They entered a small room furnished with a low coffee table and a couch with a matching chair. Liz took the chair, leaving Montgomery the couch.

"Jack tells me you're very motivated."

Montgomery stared, his wide set eyes seeming to take in all of her. Liz couldn't tell if he was coming on to her, or if he was always this unguarded.

"This is the only thing I've ever really wanted to do," he started. "I have my degree in Real Estate and have tried to do everything I can to prepare. Commercial brokerage is what I want. I'll do it somewhere, but I'd give anything to start here and run for you."

"You may get tested on that," she said.

"Try me."

Liz sat quietly in thought. Montgomery stared and waited. "How'd you like a little taste of the business this evening?" she asked.

Montgomery nodded.

"I'm picking up a client at the airport in a bit. He's coming into town to look for a new warehouse. His name's Oscar Cornblatt. Goes by Cornie. He's head of real estate for Vance Electronics. He and I are having dinner at the Ontario Hilton. We'll discuss the market and what I'll be showing him tomorrow. If you're interested, you can join us."

Montgomery shifted forward to the edge of the couch. "That would be great."

"Okay, Montgomery, you're on. I'll introduce you as brand new with the company. You won't be expected to know a thing. Just take it all in. Meet me at the bar at the Ontario Hilton at eight. If you're lucky, you may have an opportunity to make yourself useful."

*　*　*

Liz watched Cornie struggle across the tarmac, briefcase in one hand, flight bag in the other. The bottom of the bag dragged along the ground. His round shape and smooth head made him look as though the journey would have been easier if he'd rolled instead of walked. Sweat had formed above his upper lip, and even with his tie and top shirt button loosened, the excess flesh of his neck hung over his collar. The blue blazer may have looked stylish when he started the trip, but now it made him look as though he'd melt before he reached the air-conditioned refuge of the terminal building.

"Welcome to Ontario International Airport, Cornie," Liz said as she opened the door and reached for his briefcase. "Let me help."

His head tilted back slightly as he raised his eyes to meet hers. "International, my ass. Who flies in here to make it international, Colombian drug runners? I haven't had to walk across a tarmac since I visited our plant in East Jesus, New Mexico."

"Well, Cornie, it may not look like much but this airport carried more air cargo last year than any airport except Memphis, and that's because Memphis is the home of Federal Express. You want glamour or a distribution center?" Liz asked.

Cornblatt walked past her into the terminal building.

"Do we need to go to baggage claim?" she asked.

"This is it. I don't plan to be here long. Now get me to the hotel, a bath and a tall scotch."

Neither spoke as they crossed the tiled floor of the terminal. Only the staccato click of Liz's heels added to the general din. Liz's white, four-door Lexus sat at the curb. She opened the trunk and Cornblatt tossed in his travel bag.

Liz handed him back the briefcase. "Is the information I sent you in here?"

"I'm not going to need any of that until tomorrow morning," Cornblatt protested.

Liz shut the trunk, leaving him holding the bag. "Hop in."

The late afternoon sun behind them cast long shadows as they accelerated away. "I won't work you too hard before the bath and the drink. But I want you to see the Boswell building, so we can discuss it over dinner."

Cornblatt jerked his shoulders around. "Bath, scotch, business. In that order, Liz."

Liz chuckled. "Cornie, I'm telling you, it's the building you're going to end up in. It's perfect. Besides," she said as she turned off the highway, "it's on the way to the hotel."

They drove for a mile down a wide boulevard lined with concrete warehouses. Big warehouses. The single story walls rose almost forty feet and ran back from the street for as much as a quarter-mile. Monoliths with a few windows but rows of truck doors cut in their sides.

"You ever see them build one of these, Cornie?" Liz asked. "They pour all those concrete panels on the ground. Then they come in with a crane—big construction crane—and pull them all upright and hold them together with the roof. One day the site's flat as a parking lot, and the next day one of these monsters is up."

Cornie shook his head. "California," he snorted. "Everything's different. Everywhere else they use steel structures. Even warehouses are different in 'La La Land.'"

"Not everything, Cornie." Liz gave him a knowing smile, slowed the Lexus and turned into a paved yard some two hundred feet wide and at least three times as deep. Brand new warehouses stood on either side. Truck doors from both buildings faced onto the yard where she stopped. "And speaking of monsters," Liz pointed to the building on their left, "that one's yours."

Cornblatt's trained eye took it all in quickly.

"Everything you wanted, Cornie—good clearance in the warehouse, rail served and plenty of truck-high doors. We're less than a mile from three different freeways leading to anywhere in Southern California and you're within sight of the air freight terminal. Best of all, you can steal it. Boswell is in big financial trouble. He's got to do a deal or lose the whole thing."

For the first time since his arrival Cornblatt looked interested. "You got the key?"

"Of course I've got the key," Liz answered. "But let's not take too long inside."

Cornblatt looked at her quizzically.

"I'm interviewing a new runner. Just met him today. I've taken the liberty of asking him to join us for drinks and dinner at the Hilton," she explained. "I'm very interested to see what you think of him."

Cornblatt smiled furtively as he stepped out of the car.

*   *   *

Liz stopped just inside the entrance to the Hilton's Executive Room to allow her eyes to adjust to the darkness. Montgomery slid off his stool and walked across the bar toward her. The grey worsted suit draped gracefully down his slender frame.

"Didn't Mr. Cornblatt make it?" Montgomery asked.

"He's here. He just wanted to go to his room and freshen up," Liz explained. "He'll join us for dinner. Did you make us a reservation?"

"No. I didn't know you wanted me—"

"No matter," she interrupted. "Miss," Liz flagged down the hostess. "Bring my friend's drink to the dining room, and have the check sent over."

She led Montgomery across the lobby to Chez Paul's.

"Three for dinner," Liz commanded the maitre d'. "We'd like a very private table."

"The corner is available, Miss." He indicated a darkened table away from the kitchen door.

"That will be fine. Mr. Cornblatt will be joining us shortly. Please direct him."

Liz ordered a bottle of Caymus Cabernet Sauvignon. After the waiter poured it, she held her glass toward Montgomery. "To opportunity," Liz toasted.

He clinked his glass with hers, and then sipped.

Liz scowled. "You don't like it?"

Montgomery snapped erect as his eyes searched her face. "No. No," he stammered. "It's fine. Good."

"You don't seem to like it," she let her expression soften, but still pinned him with her stare.

"I'm just not much of a drinker," he apologized.

"Well, that's gotta change," Liz insisted as she twirled the stem of her glass. "If you're gonna sell to these guys, you're gonna have to learn to drink with them."

Montgomery smiled weakly, raised his glass mechanically and swallowed half of it. "Burrrrr," he shivered and shook his head until his hair fell into his eyes.

"That's better," she smiled and sipped.

Montgomery fixed her with his brown eyes as he brushed his hair back into place. "Liz, I plan to be the fastest student you've ever had."

"Why the hurry?"

"I have to learn fast to start fast. And I plan to start fast."

"First guy in your class to buy a new BMW?" Liz teased.

"I wish," he grinned as he took another drink. "No, in my case, it's to pay off the mortgage."

"You own a house, Montgomery?" She picked up the bottle and refilled his glass.

"Not me. It's Mom's." He raised his glass and somberly studied the blood red liquid. "She got sick last year. She's okay now but has no strength to work. We're not sure if or when she will again."

"Glad she's better," Liz said. "Is she getting workers' comp?"

"Oh, yeah. But it doesn't cover much. We're behind on the mortgage." He lifted his eyes and his expression as well. "I'm motivated. Money comes soon or Mom's on the street," he delivered the line with a gallows humor grin.

Liz raised her glass to him again. "Like I said, to opportunity. You'll just have to make sure you don't miss the first one that comes along."

"Amen to that," Montgomery added as he again clinked glasses.

"Toasting without the guest of honor?" Cornblatt asked as he arrived. He was all smiles and goodwill as he joined them. He had showered, shaved and changed shirts. His after-shave smelled of musk.

"Oscar Cornblatt, meet Montgomery Pierce," Liz introduced the two men.

"Pleased to meet you, Mr. Cornblatt."

Cornblatt held onto the offered hand, "Cornie, please. It's my pleasure to meet you as well." Looking at Liz he added, "You didn't tell me he was such a striking young man."

Montgomery removed his hand and looked uncomfortable.

"Cornie, we have a bottle of cabernet. Would you care to join us, or do you prefer that tall scotch you mentioned earlier?"

"I think I'll take the tall scotch now. Maybe some wine later."

After the scotch arrived and they had ordered, Liz commented, "What did you think of the Boswell building?"

"Are we going to talk business?" Cornblatt looked around the table. "Okay, Montgomery, what do you think of the building?"

Montgomery looked to Liz, but she said nothing. "Cornie, I don't even know the building. Liz invited me along to learn a bit. But I do know Liz's reputation, and if she says it's the right building at the right price, I'm sure it's so."

Liz allowed a small smile toward Montgomery.

Cornie laughed out loud. "Where do you find them, Liz? These bright, delicious young men with a flair for doing whatever advances the deal? This one's a gem." Cornblatt grinned warmly at Montgomery and patted the back of his hand.

Montgomery pulled his hand away and put it in his lap.

"I'm glad you approve, Cornie. And I'm sure Montgomery does, too," she said.

The waiter arrived, busboy in tow, and served their dinners. "I think I'll have that glass of cabernet now," Cornie commented to the waiter. "Montgomery's glass is empty. Pour him another, and bring another bottle to keep us going."

"I'm fine," Montgomery announced, but Cornblatt motioned and the waiter refilled the glasses.

They progressed through dinner and the second bottle of wine slowly.

"Liz, this afternoon you said I could steal the building. But you never mentioned price," Cornblatt commented.

Liz cut into her roast beef but left the piece on her plate. "The last buildings that sold were at thirty dollars per foot. But nothing's selling. Prices are dropping. Boswell's asking twenty-nine. I think the real number is twenty-six, maybe twenty-seven. At twenty-six dollars a foot the building sells for five million two." She picked up her fork and chewed. Cornblatt said nothing. "That's one hell of a deal!" Liz finally commented.

"Okay, Liz, it's high on the list. Tomorrow we can look around at the rest of the market, and see if that's the best." Cornblatt pushed back his plate and sighed. "Montgomery, will you be joining us?"

Montgomery wavered from side to side momentarily. As he righted himself his expression lifted with surprise. "Gee, Cornie, I hadn't even thought of that." He gave a hopeful look across the table. "Only if Liz wants me to."

Liz finished her last bite and set down her fork. "Anyone want a cup of coffee?"

"Or an after dinner drink? Maybe a port?" Cornblatt added.

"Coffee for me," Montgomery said. "And if you two will excuse me, I need to use the men's room." He pushed back from the table and walked across the restaurant on noticeably wobbly legs.

Liz leaned across the table toward Cornblatt. "Cornie, I really want to agree on this Boswell deal this evening."

"Liz, whatever is your hurry?"

"This is the right building. It's not only the best building, it's perfect. If you were building it for yourself, it's what you'd build. And the price couldn't be better. There's no reason for you and me to get up at the crack of dawn, and spend the entire day running around in the heat to prove the point. Let's just do it."

Cornblatt sat back in his chair, picked up his wine goblet, twirled it and then held the glass high between the light and his eye. "Nice wine. Nice legs." He paused. "I can get up in the morning, Liz."

Liz poured cream into her coffee, stirred for a moment, and then took a tentative sip. "Cornie, if you had a good reason not to get up so early, could we agree?"

Cornblatt arched an eyebrow.

"Suppose you got lucky tonight and didn't get to sleep until the wee hours. Would that be enough to convince you?" she asked.

"Keep talking."

"I'll seal the deal with Montgomery." She arched an eyebrow. "You like him, don't you?"

Cornblatt grinned wickedly. He picked up his port, took a sip and rolled it on his tongue. He sat the glass down and licked one little drop from the corner of his mouth. "He agrees; I agree."

"He'll agree," she said. "You go on up to your room. I'll send him up to join you."

Cornie smiled. Little beads of sweat popped out above his upper lip.

"Go on now," she urged him. "It's best if you're gone before he comes back."

Cornie got up quickly. Liz reached toward him. "Give me your room key."

With a knowing smile, he handed her the key and left.

"Meet you here for lunch," Liz called after him.

After a few minutes Montgomery returned. He looked surprised. "Cornie leave?"

"He's gone up to his room."

"Long flight, and too much to drink," Montgomery speculated.

Liz looked at him firmly. "Sit down Montgomery. Let's talk." Montgomery reached for his chair across the table from Liz. "No, not there. Here, beside me." Liz patted the unused seat to her left. Montgomery complied.

"So how'd I do tonight?" he asked.

"Night's not over," she responded. "That's what I want to talk to you about."

Montgomery looked at her with the unguarded expression she had seen earlier in the day.

"What do you think of Cornie?" she asked.

"Nice enough man." Montgomery looked perplexed. "Why?"

"Earlier today you said you'd do anything to get on as my runner. I said you might be tested. You're about to be."

Montgomery's face lifted into a smile. "I'm ready."

Liz looked directly into Montgomery's eyes. "Sleep with him."

Montgomery's eyes seemed to enlarge. She saw his throat constrict as he swallowed. When he spoke, his voice had an edge of hysteria in it. "It's… it's a joke, right?"

She kept her voice hypnotically soothing. "No, Montgomery, it's not."

"You're crazy," he choked as he rocked his chair back away from her.

She waited to see if he'd run. "He likes you, Montgomery. You're going to seal the Boswell deal."

He rocked his chair forward and leaned across the table toward her. "I'm not gay, Liz, and I'm not that drunk."

"Montgomery, let me see if I can explain this in a way you'll understand," she spoke slowly and softly. "You do this and tomorrow you're hired by ACRE as Liz Peterson's new runner. You work for me for a year, and you learn what I know and who I know. Your career will be on the rocket ship to riches you've always wanted."

His eyes blazed with disbelief and fear.

After waiting a moment she continued. "You don't do this and not only will you not be hired by ACRE, but I will personally see to it that everyone in the business knows that you got drunk at dinner, insulted a client and blew a big deal. No one will hire you. You can find another way to get through life and kiss your dreams good-bye."

The disbelief had left his face but the fear remained.

"Besides, Montgomery," she continued, "it's not so bad. All you have to do is suck the man's cock, and maybe take it up your ass. Neither of those are all that unpleasant a task." She smiled a conspiratorial smile. "And that's the opinion of someone who doesn't have a prostate. You might find it's kinda fun."

He still didn't speak, but his eyes became guarded. She could no longer read them. "You naïve little shit," she spat. "You think it's all hard work and good intentions. Get a fucking clue."

He jerked back as though struck.

"Everyone pays dues." She spoke harshly, enunciating each word slowly. "Everyone who succeeds. It's time for you to pay yours."

Liz held the room key before him. "What is it going to be? Career or no career? Take the key or get the fuck out."

He struggled. She watched. Finally, he reached forward and placed his fingers around the key. They were tentative. She didn't let go. She wasn't going make this too easy. He had to be committed before she let go. She just looked at him, her face as blank of expression as she could make it. She felt his fingers tighten on the key. When his grasp was firm, she gave him a small enigmatic smile and let go.

He took the key, rose and walked from the room.

She let out a long sigh, and for a moment sank deeply into her chair, relaxed. She drained the last of Cornblatt's port. Without looking over her shoulder, she demanded, "Check!"

CHAPTER 9

The Investigation

"HI, BOSS. You look like you've taken to this corner office," Mike Grazlyn said as he stuck his head through the open doorway. Jack looked up and saw Mike's broad face covered by a toothy smile. The coarse black hair hung in his eyes. Mike ran a hand across his forehead and forced it back into place.

"If I didn't, I'd blame you. So I'm happy for both of us that it worked out," Jack beamed back. "Come on in. Talk to me."

"I hear Liz did it again," Mike said.

"That she did. She was in early this afternoon with a Purchase and Sale agreement on one of Max Boswell's buildings," Jack responded as he motioned to the chair.

Mike threw his bulky frame down. "I heard that. I didn't hear who the fuck the buyer was."

"Vance."

"Big electronics firm?"

Jack nodded. "Liz represented them. CB Commercial represented Boswell. She'll make about six bits on the deal after she splits with the house. She's gonna make it tough for the rest of you big hitters to keep up."

"I'm here to ask you to help me do just that."

"I'd love to. Like it says up there on the Mission Statement," Jack pointed to a blank spot on the wall behind him, "'The Sales

Manager's job is to provide assistance and support in the development and successful implementation of individual brokers' market plans.'"

Mike looked from the empty wall to Jack. "Mission Statement? What fuckin' Mission Statement?"

"The Mission Statement I promised Miles I'd put up there." Jack jerked a thumb at the wall. "I know what it says. I just haven't gotten around to getting it printed and framed." Both men laughed. "How can I help?"

"You know Dick Thompson." Mike brushed a heavy lock of black bangs out of his eyes.

"Yeah, I represented him while I was with So Cal Commercial. He was US Equities' asset manager in Los Angeles. What about him?"

"He's just joined National Commerce Bank. I'd like to meet him," Mike answered.

"That's easy enough. But why?"

"Patch Patterson's been kicked upstairs by NCB. Thompson is going to be handling their product in Southern California now."

"What product?" Jack asked. "NCB's a lender. They don't own anything."

"That's about to change. They've foreclosed on the Cunningham Project. NCB's not interested in owning all that industrial shit Cunningham built by the courthouse. They hired your buddy Thompson to turn those turkeys into cash."

"So you meet my old friend Dick Thompson, and convince him you're the guy who can sell them all, turkeys or not."

"Somethin' like that."

Jack stared out the window at the San Bernardino Mountains disappearing into the haze. He turned back to the man he'd helped guide into the business almost fifteen years ago. "What do you say to convince him of that?"

"The usual stuff." Mike's answer was instantaneous.

Jack's response was slower in coming. "Like what?"

ALPHA MALE

Mike scratched his head. "We'll sell this stuff quicker and for more money than anyone around." He delivered the line with the enthusiasm of a student with the correct answer.

Jack looked out the window again, and while still studying the hazy landscape said, "You'll go down like the Wide World of Sports ski jumper."

"What?" Mike furrowed his brow quizzically.

Again, Jack turned his attention from the view outside, and focused on the big man across from him. "Mike, these bank guys are different than developers. Developers make their living balancing perceived risk against real risk. Right?" Jack waited for agreement.

"Yeah," Mike said. "They know the market as well as we do. They're all a bunch of riverboat gamblers. They see a change in the market, and they react. They don't wait."

"Exactly my point." Jack spoke more rapidly now. "They think like us, or maybe we think like them. But bankers are different. Bad decisions are not tolerated. It's okay to miss an opportunity, but it's not okay to take a bad one. There's no premium on speed. These guys study everything. They're slow—very slow. And methodical." Jack leaned forward until his palms rested on the desk. "Their whole culture says, 'play it safe; don't stick your neck out.' And since the savings and loans have started to fall, federal regulators are on them like stink on shit."

"What's this got to do with selling Thompson's project?"

"Look," Jack continued, "our usual approach won't work with institutional types. If you go to NCB and say, 'You're taking property back. You should let us sell it for you because American Corporate Real Estate is the oldest, biggest, best firm around. Besides we make all the deals in the market,' it isn't going to fly."

"Why not?" Mike demanded. "It's true."

"NCB doesn't care if it's true. They may say their first priority is to sell those buildings as soon as they foreclose, but it's not true. They may even think it's true, but it isn't."

"Bullshit," Mike exclaimed. "Of course they want to sell them."

Jack settled into his chair. "Oh, they want their money back all right." He spoke slowly now. "But there's something they want even more."

Mike arched an eyebrow, but didn't speak.

"They want to be damn certain that no one—not the president of the bank, or an inspector from the Office of the Controller of the Currency, or the attorney for a dissident shareholders group, no one—can prove they made a mistake. Decisions made by Dick Thompson don't have to be correct, but they sure as hell have to be supportable."

Mike's expression lifted until his face beamed. His new understanding was so clearly apparent, Jack could almost see the last piece of the jigsaw puzzle snap into place inside Mike's head.

Jack moved forward in his chair. "Can you figure out how to make that happen?"

"You betcha! I'll devise a scheme to make Dick Thompson feel like he's gonna live and thrive long enough to become the chairman of NCB—or at least to leave with his pension fully fuckin' vested."

Jack knew he would too. "I'll set up lunch."

Mike nodded and lifted himself out of the chair.

As he walked out the door Mike collided with a somewhat flustered Irene. Her dark curls bounced as Mike caught her. "That was fun. Wanna do it again?" he asked.

"Mike, behave," Irene commanded. She stepped around him and turned to Jack. "There's a Deputy Woodward at the front desk. San Bernardino County Sheriff's Department. He says he wants to see you."

"Oh, oh. Time for me to leave," said Mike. "One of your charges has done it up good this time, Jack." He smiled at Irene. "Might be fun if it was you." He left before she could respond.

Jack and Irene looked at each other. "Show the deputy in, Irene."

Deputy Woodward covered his potbelly with an aging tweed jacket. Khaki slacks with a tattersall shirt and solid blue wool necktie cut square across the bottom completed his ensemble. He had a head full of sandy tousled hair and wire-rim glasses. "Thanks for taking a moment, Mr. Kendrick. I don't want to cause any alarm. I just need to get your help with a couple of questions."

"Fine by me," Jack answered. "About what?"

"Did you know a Montgomery Pierce?"

"Met him yesterday. He was here for a job interview."

"And that was the first time you'd met him?" the deputy continued.

"Yes, we spoke for thirty or forty minutes in the middle of the afternoon," Jack answered again. "I left him sitting in our waiting room."

"Waiting for who?"

"For one of our sales people, Liz Peterson. He was to interview with her as well," said Jack. "Deputy Woodward, you said, 'did I know Montgomery'. Has something happened to him?"

"Last night—early this morning really—he died. We found your business card in his pocket and thought you might be able to help."

"My God," Jack's pulse jumped. "What happened?"

"His Celica hit the Jurupa overpass to the I-15 freeway. He died at the scene. What was his mood when he left you? Did he seem happy? Stable?"

"Upbeat as a young man with a new diploma on a job interview could be," Jack answered. "Was he drinking?"

"We won't know until we get the autopsy report."

"Autopsy?" Jack knew his face showed surprise. "Why an autopsy?"

Deputy Woodward pulled a small notebook from his jacket

pocket. He licked the end of his thumb and thumbed through several pages, and then reviewed his notes. "The engine of Pierce's Celica ended up in the back seat. Best estimate is he was going eighty when he hit the overpass."

Jack could read nothing in the deputy's expression. "He was going real fast, and he hit the overpass and he died. That's awful." He paused. "But why an autopsy?"

"Eighty's about as fast as that car will go. Plus there weren't any skid marks. He never touched the brakes. When there's no attempt to brake, suicide is a possibility we have to investigate before the coroner can decide the cause of death. That requires an autopsy."

"I understand," Jack said in a subdued voice.

"Here's my card," the deputy said, handing it to Jack. "If you think of anything else, call me." He rose to go. "Oh, one last thing. Could I get Liz Peterson's number? I'd like to talk with her."

Jack hastily scribbled Liz's number on a message slip and handed it to the deputy. "Would you call me when your investigation is complete? I'd like to know."

Deputy Woodward nodded as he left.

*   *   *

"My love, you are very pensive this evening." Lorna clutched at his arm with both hands and looked up at him.

His response was a warm smile. He didn't speak or stop walking. Ahead of them the Manhattan Beach Pier ran some two hundred yards across the sand and into the ocean. Perched at the end stood the small rounded structure that housed the Roundhouse Marine Museum. The concrete ribbon they strolled along was paralleled by another some five yards below them. The lower path was reserved for the helmeted bicycle riders flying past. Above them The Strand was lined by homes. Some of them were wooden beach bungalows dating from the 'twenties and some steel and glass architectural extravaganzas. But all had in common million dollar plus values.

He walked slowly enjoying the beach, the walk and her warmth.

"It's that boy, isn't it?"

"Mostly," he answered. "Mostly."

She didn't speak, knowing she'd prodded all she needed to.

"My mind keeps going back to him," Jack finally started. "He was alive, vibrant and in my office. And then dead. Surreal. Like he never really was. Just a movie."

A brave soul, or just one ignorant of the law, threw a frisbee out across the beach, and the terrier streaked after it. They both watched as the dog missed it in the air but picked it up off the ground and trotted across the beach and to its master sitting on the porch of one of the old wooden ones. Back, safe with the frisbee and without a "No Dogs On Beach" citation.

They started to stroll again and Jack started again. "But it wasn't a movie. That boy was real."

"So did he do it?"

"Kinda sounds that way, doesn't it," he answered. "But why?"

"Honey, he had lots of sadness about him. No dad, sick mom and big financial pressures. Maybe it was all just too much."

"Maybe," Jack agreed. "Maybe, but he also had a vision. He felt like he was at the beginning of something, not the end."

"You said he felt weak. Maybe he was too weak to begin."

"Maybe. Lots of maybes."

They were silent as they walked into the gathering dark.

"Tell me something good," she said in an upbeat tone.

"Like, I love you."

"Yeah, that's good." She squeezed his hand. "But I meant about work. Lift my mood."

He thought for a minute. "Mike's on to something big, and I think I can help put it together for him." His stride extended a few inches now.

"Tell," she said.

As they turned up the hill toward home, Jack told her the

whole tale of Mike figuring out that Cunningham was bound to fail and then positioning himself where he'd be needed.

As they stopped at the light, waiting to cross Pacific Coast Highway, Lorna asked, "Mike figured all that out?"

"Sure did. Clever, huh?"

"And Liz didn't?"

Jack turned and peered into her deep brown eyes. "No, this time Mike seems to be in there all alone."

"I wouldn't count on it," Lorna advised. "That woman is very good at positioning herself in the middle of things."

CHAPTER 10

Between a Rock and a Hard Place

FROM THE thirty-seventh floor of the National Commerce Bank Plaza, the streets of Los Angeles took on an ever-hazier patina as Jack looked south toward the harbor. The June sun glaring up at him from the smog below was almost as dazzling as the sheen on the long, polished wood table that took up the center of the room.

"Jack, ol' buddy, good of you to come all the way in," a voice boomed behind him.

Jack turned to see a jacketless Dick Thompson march through the double-doored entrance to the room. His thinning blond hair seem to trail behind and the buttons on his shirt gapped over his expanded chest as he turned to stride the length of the room and get around the table to his guest.

Jack turned and matched him stride for stride along the length of the table. They rounded the end of the table at the same time and engaged in a lusty shaking of hands.

"Couldn't you find a suitably large meeting place," Jack teased.

"Thought you'd get a kick out of the board room. Besides, it's part of the story I want to tell."

"I'm all ears."

"Coffee? Water? Any of that stuff, buddy?"

"Coffee. Black."

Thompson pointed at the chair next to Jack. "Sit. I'll get us some."

Jack sat. Thompson turned to the phone on a table in the corner, spoke a few words, and then sat in the large armchair at the head of the table.

"It happened right here, Jack." Thompson nodded his head down the length of the table. "This is where we took back Cunningham's project."

"Foreclosed."

"Oh, no. He gave us the deed in lieu of foreclosure. By the time our attorneys finished with him, he was damn glad to give back all those vacant warehouses we'd loaned him the money to build." Thompson's ruddy complexion got even redder as he laughed. "Shit, he was pleased we didn't take away his house, his cars, boats and all his other toys."

A young man with a tray in his hand and a deferent demeanor came in the door and made the long walk to the head of the table. They waited and watched.

"Mr. Thompson."

"Just set the tray here, Domingo. Thank you."

The attendant complied and left.

"Black you said?" Thompson asked.

Jack nodded as Thompson poured from the silver pot into a china cup embossed with the National Commerce Bank logo.

"Thanks." Jack sipped. "So what then?"

"You know Patch Patterson?"

Jack nodded again.

"He ran the meeting. Tends to babble. At least he did that day."

Thompson stopped and poured himself a cup and then gulped at the steaming brew. The cup looked too small for his hand.

"It didn't matter," he continued. "He was only here to take the project back. Once that was done, I knew the bank would give the whole damn thing to me to clean up." Thompson looked directly at Jack, an expression of disgust on his face. "To salvage what cash he could from the disaster Patch, and his good old boy relationship with Cunningham, created for NCB."

Thompson paused and then his face lit with a sardonic grin. "You know Cunningham has his monogram on both the breast pocket and the cuff of his shirts?"

"Little bit of ego," Jack speculated and shared the smile.

Thompson's mobile face suddenly became reflective. "Maybe the bastard deserves that much ego."

"How so?"

"Robert Cunningham was one hell of a big fish for a long time," Thompson explained. "He was the guy who convinced San Bernardino County to build the new courthouse in the middle of nowhere. The middle of nowhere, where Cunningham just happened to own all the contiguous land. For a long time after that, he made a lot of money developing office buildings for all those attorneys, bondsmen and recording companies who needed space right next to the courthouse."

"And it would have worked if the fool had stopped there and not built all that industrial space," Jack finished the thought.

"Yeah, exactly." Thompson paused and his face again took on a reflective aspect. "But I wonder, ol' buddy, who had been the bigger fool? Cunningham for thinking that because he managed to lease office space he'd be able to lease industrial buildings too, or NCB for loaning him the money to turn those pipe-dreams into reality?"

Jack let the rhetorical question hang in the air.

"It doesn't much matter now," Thompson added.

"What does matter now?" Jack asked.

"That I recover a bunch of NCB's cash out of this fiasco, and that I do it damn fast."

"And that's why you asked me up here?"

"Yeah, ol' buddy, you're part of this," Thompson almost beamed, and then instantly turned serious. "But you're not going to like your part."

"What do you want?"

"I want you to do what every sales manager dreads."

Jack knew he didn't need to speak.

Thompson continued, "I'm going to make you pick between a couple of your brokers."

"Let me guess." Jack smiled, understanding now. "You've got a couple of my sales people pounding on your door about all those little Cunningham buildings?"

"Bull's eye! Now do you want to see if you can guess who they are?" Thompson teased.

"I know Mike Grazlyn is one because I set up your original meeting, and Mike's too bright to miss the obvious."

"So far, so good," Dick said. "Who else?"

"I'll guess Liz Peterson has been yanking your chain."

"No, you're wrong. It's Paul Jensen."

"Jensen? I didn't know he was focused on small buildings. But the whole bunch will total over—what, twenty-five or thirty million dollars? That's enough to get Paul's attention." Jack felt irked he'd allowed his surprise to show, even to an old friend.

"It's more like twenty-five million, but I'd be happy if someone could get me thirty," Dick continued. "Paul and his son have been in here off and on for almost two months, long before anyone else. They started out talking to Patch about the project. When the file came to me, they were in my office the next day. Been very helpful with market information, that sort of thing." He paused. "Paul tells me he does all the deals."

Jack ignored the hint of sarcasm in Thompson's tone. "How far along is this process? Is it time for a formal presentation?"

"Not yet. But I'm not putting myself in the position of pissing off any big brokers. I'm going to make you the bad guy. I'll only hear one presentation from each of the major brokerage firms. You pick the broker to make it for ACRE."

"Okay. I'll have a few conversations, and I'll call you back." He took a last drink from the china cup and stood up. "Maybe we can meet at the project. I'd like to see it."

Thompson stood as well. "Good idea. Let's do it later in the week." A grin popped out on Thompson's face that was almost infectious. "In fact I can stop by your office and pick you up. I'd love to meet that receptionist of yours. She's polite, smart and efficient. A hard combination to find."

"She's pretty as she sounds, and built like the Pet of the Year." Jack let himself share in Thompson's smile. "Now I know you'll show up."

They both laughed.

"I can show myself out. Besides," Jack added, "you look perfect in that chair.

The two men shook hands and then Jack took the long walk along the table to the big double-doors.

Thompson watched him go. When Jack was out of the room he involuntarily grimaced. Selling off a project this big would be like chumming for shark. There were millions to be made in commissions. Word of the foreclosure would be a trail of blood in the water. They'd all start circling, and just like sharks the most dangerous would rush up out of the depths to rip at the prize. It would be exciting to watch, but he'd have to be careful not to get eaten.

*   *   *

He relaxed into the depths of the high-backed seat as he accelerated onto the freeway. The meeting had presented exciting prospects. Selling all those little buildings would be a lot of work, but it would generate well over a million dollars in fees to the firm. But there were risks—for him. Picking between star brokers would be a hot potato.

As Miles Preston had said, "It's tough for a manager, who's a hundred-thousand-dollar expense item, to direct someone who's a million-dollar income item." Miles will have to be part of this.

* * *

Jack walked across the bullpen to the big corner office where he'd first interviewed with Miles.

"Got a minute?" Jack tapped on the doorframe.

Miles always paused a moment before responding. At first Jack had thought Miles might be hard of hearing. He wasn't. It was just a little trick of his to leave a person standing for a moment. His way of reminding you who was boss.

Miles finally looked up from his paperwork. "What do you need, Jack?"

Jack spent ten minutes explaining the history of the Cunningham project, those involved and Dick Thompson's call.

"I'll talk to Paul Jensen and Mike Grazlyn tomorrow. You want to participate?"

The corners of Miles' mouth showed just the hint of a wry smile. "This Thompson fellow asked you to do it. You should do what our client wants."

"Fine by me, Miles. But the loser is going to come to you. We need to be of one mind on this."

"If mom says no, then go ask dad. I suspect you're right," Miles said. "Still this is up to you. You decide."

"Okay, but when the loser comes to you, just remember this is my call," Jack said and set his face with determination.

"Good luck, Jack," Miles said.

Jack didn't see either Mike or Paul as he crossed the office. "Irene, are either Paul or Mike in?" Jack asked as he passed the switchboard.

"Both checked out," came the cheery response.

"Tell both of them I want to see him ASAP."

* * *

"You wanted to talk to me?"

The booming baritone voice behind Jack startled him. He

missed the cup, and hot coffee streamed over his thumb and onto the formica counter top. "Damn!" He set the styrofoam cup on the counter and waved his left hand to cool it. Jack looked over his shoulder into Paul Jensen's deep green eyes. "Do you always walk so quietly?" The sardonic smile showing at the corners of Paul's mouth annoyed him as much as his burned thumb.

"Mostly, yes." Paul pulled several paper towels out of the rack over the sink and held them toward Jack. "Want to wipe off the counter top?"

Jack took the towels.

"I'll pour for both of us," Paul said as he picked up the pot and filled two cups. "You want to talk here, or in your office?" Paul offered one of the cups.

"My office," Jack walked past Paul, out of the break room and to his office.

When they were seated across the desk from one another, Jack began. "I understand you and Brent have been calling on NCB and are trying to list the Cunningham project."

Paul openly studied Jack's face for a moment. "It didn't take a genius to figure out that Cunningham wasn't going to get the prices he was asking and was eventually going to lose everything. Patch Patterson's an old friend. He and I started talking months ago. If he hadn't been promoted, we'd have the listing by now." Paul picked up his cup, blew over the top and took a sip. "He'll still have a say, but we may be forced into a beauty contest before it's over."

"That's what I hear." Jack rubbed his reddening thumb into his right palm. "How much say do you think Patch has?"

"He's the boss."

"You sure?"

"You know something I don't?" Paul asked.

"General stuff," Jack answered. "A lot of our old friends at institutions are losing control to a new breed. Finance types."

Paul arched an eyebrow.

"You sure Patch hasn't just been moved aside?" Jack continued.

"Well, NCB sure as hell needs someone who can make deals on those buildings." Paul pulled himself forward in the chair. His jaw muscles tightened a bit. "This Dick Thompson guy who's in charge now tells me you two know each other. Can he do it?"

"Oh, he can do it. I've watched him do dozens of deals." Jack took a drink. His thumb no longer burned. "But he's one of those bean counters you mention so disdainfully. He does everything by the spreadsheet. Every decision is related to the project proforma." Jack paused. "But you asked the wrong question. The real question is can you do it?"

After a moment of obvious reflection, Paul's face suddenly broke out into a huge smile and his green eyes began to twinkle. "It's time you and I got to know each other better. I'm meeting Brent later in the day at a friend's corral over in Rialto. We're gonna have a little fun. Why don't you join us? We can get to know each other a bit. Sling a little bull, or maybe the other way around."

* * *

Jack wasn't entirely comfortable. The jeans were just a little too bulky for comfort, but the boots were the real problem. They were too big, so he had to curl his toes under when he walked to keep them from slapping. It made his gait odd and a little uncomfortable. He'd kept on his own white shirt, but the rest of the gear was Paul's. Well, it was that or wear the suit and that wouldn't work. Bullriding was Paul's game. He'd accepted the invitation, now he was going to have to accept a little discomfort.

But mostly he was fascinated. The bull had been forced into a wooden crate that appeared a size too small. The crate was about six feet tall and constructed of fence boards. He'd climbed three boards high up the outside of the crate and was looking down at the broad brown back of what had to be the biggest bull he'd ever seen. Well, he hadn't seen that many bulls, but this thing was huge. Took up the whole crate. Head down and motionless as it was, it could have been stuffed. But as Brent eased down onto the beast, a small shudder ran across the skin covering its haunches sending two flies to wing. The beast made no sound and the stillness was frightening. Like standing in the silent eye of a hurricane knowing destruction was close at hand.

The creature was so broad that Brent had to force his booted legs between it and the sides of the crate just to straddle the thing. As Brent eased his weight from his arms and sat on the broad back, the beast made no motion. No kicking or stomping. No vain or useless thrashing. Just a snort and an unseeable, but palpable, tensing of the huge muscles gave prelude to the explosion to come.

Brent patted the massive shoulder in front of him just where the blades met. A crude rope harness was already there. He slid his left hand under it, palm up, wrapped the loose end twice around his hand and then tucked the remainder of the rope back under the harness.

Preparations completed, Brent raised his right hand high over head. It was a gesture the starter of a race might use. He looked at his father, then slowly turned his eyes to Jack, and grinned. Finally, he looked down at the cowboy standing inside the corral with his hand on the latch to the gate and said, "Cut 'er loose."

The gate swung open and the beast exploded into the corral. He led with his head and shoulders, throwing left out the gate and kicking his rears. He continued a left turn so tight he threatened to come back into the crate. Each time he turned his massive rear quarters kicked up off the ground.

Brent whooped with glee and each time the bull landed he pulled himself forward on the rope.

Paul was screaming, "Hang on 'em. Hang on." And then, "Oh, Christ he's coming back right."

The bull had thrown his head to the left again in the ever tightening circle, but this time he didn't go around. With massive power, the beast turned right instead, snapping Brent, who'd been leaning into the turn, back out. For the first time his rope arm extended and it looked like he'd fly off, but as the bull bucked again the energy of the rising haunches carried the rider forward, and with an incredible display of arm and abdominal strength, he pulled himself back upright. The bull ran forward across the ring bucking as he went, but the rider stayed up.

The clear clean sound of the bell got a whoop from Paul and the wranglers attending. Brent swung his right leg forward over the bull's withers, pulled free from the rope and jumped.

He fell as he landed and two cowboys immediately ran toward the bull's head. But the beast ignored them both and loped across the corral to the chute leading out of the far side.

Jack was speechless.

Paul turned to him with a smile as wide as the bull's back. "Exciting enough?" And he jumped off the crate to the ground.

Jack followed. "Shit, Paul. Just shit. Aren't you afraid that thing is gonna' stomp him once he comes off?"

"Not a silly question, Jack. In fact, most riders don't get hurt being thrown, it's getting stomped on after that gets 'em. But these practice bulls aren't mean at all. To most of 'em it's just a job." His green eyes flashed and he put an arm around Jack and pounded his back. "But you did ask me a silly question earlier today."

Jack beamed back, "And what was that?"

Paul pulled himself back up on the fence until he was sitting on the top board. Jack followed and saw a very pleased Brent Jensen walking across the corral toward them. Paul waved at his son, clearly proud of his courage and skill. He looked back at Jack. "Your silly question was, 'can you do it?'"

Jack was jerked back to reality.

"Remember?" Paul asked.

"Yeah, I remember." He scowled. Jack knew where this was going. Schoolboy stuff about who was tougher, more able. "My dick is bigger than yours." Schoolboy stuff, maybe, but powerful even now and he'd have to let Paul play it out.

Paul pointed to the horizon and swept his arm in a long arc. "Look around you, Jack. What do you see?"

Jack twisted his head and in the distance, beyond the edge of the barn-lot they occupied, the landscape was peppered with the tall concrete walls of a dozen warehouses.

"Jack, I can do it because I've been doing deals in the Inland Empire since there was nothing out here but cows, vineyards and dreams."

"And that's your answer?"

"That's my answer."

"Then you lose."

"Bull…shit," Paul snorted.

Jack waited until the color cooled in Paul Jensen's face. "Paul, whether you hear me or not is up to you, but I'm telling you Dick Thompson's going to work with someone who does business his way—by the numbers. If that's not you, you're not his guy."

"I think Patch will help me there. He can vouch for me." A smile returned to his face. "And he will."

"Patch isn't going to be any help on this one."

Paul visibly tensed.

"Dick Thompson's in complete control of this. He's told me to pick the broker to make ACRE's presentation."

Paul edged forward on the fence. His mouth curved up into a smile and his eyes held Jack's with intense focus.

He likes this, Jack thought. The old war-horse excited by the sound of battle.

Brent reached the fence, put a boot on the lower board and a hand on top and catapulted his thin muscular frame up to join them.

"Ya' did great, kid." Paul tousled the blond curls on his son's head.

"How you two doin'?" Brent asked looking pointedly from his father to Jack.

"The new boss doesn't think I got it anymore."

"Now hold on, Paul," Jack jumped in, "I…"

Brent cut him off. "We'll show 'em."

Paul grinned. "Okay, I will." He looked across the corral, stuck his little finger and his index finger in his mouth and whistled shrilly.

One of the wranglers turned toward the sound. Paul made a "come-to-me" motion with his whole arm. The cowboy pointed toward the back chute. Paul nodded his head.

Paul looked at Jack, his jaw set defiantly. "We'll see who can and who can't." He jumped down off the fence and into the corral and started across.

"Just what the hell does he plan to prove he can do?" Jack looked into the sharp features and smooth skin that made up the face of Brent Jensen.

"You'll see, Dude."

Jack had never been called Dude before, much less by an employee, and he recoiled as though struck. Well, it may not be respectful, he thought, but I am sitting on a wood fence in borrowed jeans. Not exactly a position commanding of respect. He let it slide.

Brent had neither looked away nor blinked since he spoke.

"Your dad doesn't want to waste his time working a bunch of small deals and you and I both know it." Jack thought that was appropriately abrupt as an opening gambit.

"He's part of a team. He knows every trick for pulling a deal together, and I'm the cold-calling-machine who will contact the occupant of every industrial building between here and downtown LA." Brent's expression was both haughty and arrogant. "Now, you answer a question for me."

Jack nodded.

"Who are Dad and I competing against for the right to make this presentation?"

The loud whoop popped both of their heads around just in time to see a gate across the corral fly open and a huge white bull burst into the arena. Hanging on top, left hand tied tight to the beast's withers and right hand held high, was Paul Jensen.

"My God," Jack gulped, "he's actually doing this." The last part came out in a whisper.

Brent was screaming, "Ride 'em! Ride 'em big guy!"

The bull jumped straight forward three times. Paul moved a bit further down its back with each leap, but he held on. Then the beast stopped abruptly at the end of a leap and then instantly sprung hard to the right. Paul slid further back and leaned precariously out to the left, his arm fully extended from the rope.

"Get up on, Dad! Get up!"

The white bull leaped once more hard right and Paul flew off still in a sitting position. That's how he hit the earth.

Again, two wranglers ran straight toward the bull, but again he trotted almost docilely to the open chute and out of the corral.

Paul sat still, in the position he'd landed. The wranglers reached him. He spoke to one and extended his hand. The cowboy pulled him up. He took off his hat, dusted his ass with the brim and then started slowly across the corral toward them.

"Good ride, Dad. You'll get the big bastard next time." And then without skipping a beat turned to Jack. "You didn't answer my question."

Jack looked from the slow-moving form of the father limping out of the arena to the arrogant smirk of the son. "Mike Grazlyn," he answered. "Any reason I should pick you instead of him?"

"That bull is one strong sumbitch," Paul Jensen spoke from about ten feet as he approached them.

Brent jumped down and extended his hand. "Good ride. You were on there six or seven seconds. Close."

"Close don't win no belt-buckles." Paul gave his son a wry grin. Then he looked at Jack perched on top of the fence. "There's one ready for you in that crate across the corral."

Paul's green eyes held his without compromise. Jack felt his toes wiggle inside the too-large boots. Time to see whose dick really was bigger. He jumped down into the corral. He landed flat-footed and looked up into the challenging green eyes. He could have ducked those, he thought, but that smirk on the kid is too damn much. Without a word he straightened himself to his full height, walked directly between the two of them and across the arena.

*   *   *

He leaned over the top of the crate and looked in. It was filled with immense rippling muscles and horns. No sound came from the beast. It seemed to know its mere presence represented an ominous challenge that was more terrifying for the lack of sound or motion.

"Never done this before." It was more statement than question and it was delivered with a softness that belied the hazard.

Jack looked at the wrangler on the other side of the crate and just shook his head.

"It's pretty simple really. You just ease down on top of Widow-Maker here. I'll show you how to tie into the rope and then when you say the word, I open the gate and you ride."

Jack looked at the wrangler. He was sure his tongue would clack if he tried to speak. After a long silence, Jack moved his feet up the slats in the crate, slowly climbing to the top. Once there, he straddled the sides then lowered himself onboard.

Jack had been this scared on his first night patrol in the jungles of Vietnam. His heart pounded so loudly he wasn't sure he could hear anything else. But Widow-Maker didn't move. He felt like he was sitting across the hood of an Oldsmobile. It was warm and gave no sign of threat, but what the hell was he going to hang onto if someone floored this thing. Make that when.

The wrangler was patiently wrapping his hand into the rope. "Your hand won't get stuck in there. It will come out whether you jump or fall."

Jack nodded dumbly.

"Try to stay forward. Every time he jumps, you jump forward and pull hard." And then after a pause. "Say when."

And then Jack was alone. Alone with the beast.

"Open up."

He catapulted sideways. And then forward. He threw his hand high for balance, dug in with his knees and tried to stay forward—over the withers—near the rope. His stomach muscles ached with the effort to pull back to the center, but he kept moving back and out. Further from the safety of the rope. And then he was airborne. There was no more jolting, just a sense of acceleration. His left leg hit first and collapsed immediately, and he rolled. Hard. His shoulder hit and he pitched forward and rolled again. He landed on his back but the adrenaline pulled him up and running. Running toward the fence and safety. But Widow-Maker had finished his day's work and was headed toward the barn. Jack slowed to a walk. The boots slapped.

When he reached the fence, two hands reached down for him. He took Paul's and let himself be pulled up.

Paul slapped him on the back. "Good first ride."

"Good last ride, too."

"You won't win no buckles if you don't make the eight count." Brent's grin was smug and superior. "Wanna' go again?"

"Paul, why don't you teach your son a little something about respect for his elders," Jack suggested, not recognizing the speaker. Then he swiveled his legs to the other side of the fence, hopped down, and started to the parking lot.

Both Paul and Brent jumped down after and quickly caught up.

"Jack, one thing before you leave."

He stopped and turned to face the Jensens.

"Brent tells me Mike Grazlyn is our competition on this one."

"That's right."

"You asked if there was any reason you should pick us instead of Grazlyn," Paul continued.

"Right again."

"Well there is one pretty good one."

"What's that?"

"Because neither Brent nor I have the conflict of representing the Bancroft Project right down the street," Paul answered.

Jack tried to keep his surprise from showing. Lorna once called him "newsprint face" because everything he felt showed. He'd forgotten about Bancroft. It was the only possible competition for the NCB project. Nobody was building anything. Even if someone wanted to, they couldn't find financing for the construction. No one except Kevin Bancroft. He was the contrarian and the only developer with the cash and the huevos to build. And Mike Grazlyn represented Kevin Bancroft.

"That's gonna be a factor," Jack admitted. "One I hadn't considered."

"Anything else you want to know?" Paul asked. His expression appeared triumphant. He was clearly enjoying himself.

"That's plenty for now," Jack answered. "I'll get back to you with my decision." He turned to go.

"Talked to Mike yet?" Brent asked as he walked away.

"Not yet," Jack answered over his shoulder.

"Have fun," the younger Jensen retorted.

*   *   *

Mike came into the office with his usual good-natured smile and black mop hanging in his eyes. A stack of documents an inch thick in his hand. "Well, boss, here's the deal. I've positioned myself pretty well with Thompson and I think he genuinely likes the work I've done. This," Mike waved the documents, "is the complete plan for selling all those little puppies and monitoring the work in progress with very little effort on Thompson's part." Mike dropped into the chair across the desk from Jack.

"Do you always deliver an entire speech in one breath?" Jack teased.

Mike's big hand brushed the mane of black hair out of his eyes. "Only to guys quick enough to keep up," he quipped.

Jack rubbed his face. "Mike, you're the most prepared guy

around," he said, revealing pleasure in his voice, "but you're not the only person in the office who's trying to get in front of this deal."

"Yeah," said Mike, "I figure Jensen is probably trying to work something out with Patch Patterson."

Jack paused and then said slowly, "Only one of you is going to get the chance."

"Well, we both know I'm the right guy. Paul's riding the wrong fucking horse. Thompson's gonna make this decision." Mike's face lit up with a "cat ate the canary" grin. "Can you imagine him putting up with Jensen's patronizing, 'I do all the deals' shit?" Mike cocked his head and peered quizzically, seeming to wait for Jack's expression to register agreement. When it didn't, Mike straightened. "You talk to Jensen yet?"

"I've talked to him," Jack answered. "He brought up something I need to ask you about."

"So ask?"

"Kevin Bancroft."

Mike's shoulders came forward just a bit and the flesh at the top of his nose bunched together. "What about him?" Mike made it sound casual enough.

"You represent him and his project. It competes." Jack struggled to keep a sense of finality out of his voice.

"God damn it, Jack," Mike jerked forward. "Is that what Jensen told you?"

Jack shrugged.

"Did he also tell you Kevin has yet to break ground?" Mike placed both his palms on top of Jack's desk and leaned forward until his face came within three feet of Jack's. "It will be spring before they're up. They don't compete!"

Jack pushed his chair back to increase the distance between them. "Not now, but how about then? You expect to sell two dozen buildings for NCB within six months?"

"Jack, buddy..." Mike removed his palms from the desk but

stayed on the front edge of his chair. "We do this all the time around here. I can name half a dozen projects Paul represents that compete with each other. It's not a problem."

"That's up to Dick Thompson, and he may think it is," Jack responded. "Mike, how many buildings in Bancroft's project?"

"Five."

"Five. Against five times that many at NCB," Jack mused. "Would you resign the Bancroft listing if it becomes an issue?"

"Love to, boss, but I can't." Mike's easy smile had returned. "Kevsie and I are old school chums. His dad left him some money, and I got him into this deal." Mike rose and walked to the door and stopped. He turned around, gave his sales manager a slow smile. "I can't abandon him now. You understand?" It sounded like a request for forgiveness. Then Mike's voice became firm. "And I don't expect you to abandon me either."

"What's that supposed to mean?" Jack let the edge show in his voice.

"You asked me for help once, Jack, and I gave it. Didn't I?" Mike stood square in the doorway, his bulk taking up most of the frame.

Jack almost jumped forward, caught himself, exhaled and then rose slowly. He walked around the desk and toward the door. Grazlyn didn't back away; didn't move. Jack stopped two feet in front of him looking up at the big face with the black mane hanging around it.

"You did, Mike, and I am grateful. But that won't affect my decision here." He looked up and said no more.

Mike stared back for what seemed like an eternity. "You'll ask Dick if it's a problem before you decide?"

"Yes, Mike, I'll ask."

And the big man turned and walked back across the office.

* * *

"Ever been to Africa?" Jack asked. They stood in a parking lot surrounded by unoccupied, concrete industrial buildings. The grass

needed mowing, cobwebs hung in some of the doorways, and dust
and wind-driven debris collected in the corners.

"No, ol' buddy, I haven't," Thompson answered. "Why?"

"A friend and his wife just came back. On the trip, he learned
a lesson from his guide. He said, a gazelle wakes up every morning
knowing it has to outrun the fastest lion or it will be eaten. And a
lion wakes up every morning knowing it will have to outrun the
slowest gazelle or it will starve."

"So?"

"So whether you're a lion or a gazelle, you'd better get up running."

Thompson laughed. "You a lion or a gazelle?"

"I'm not sure, but I wake up running."

They both laughed. Thompson headed across the lot and toward the nearest building. Jack followed.

"Jesus, things deteriorate fast." Thompson pointed at a ply-
wood sheet covering a broken window. "Have you made up your
mind?" he looked back at Jack and asked.

"What do you think of Paul Jensen?"

"Well he's been around forever and seems to know a lot about
the market. That's good. But there's always the question with an
old lion like Paul; will he run after those little gazelles?" Thompson delivered the line with a chuckle. "This is a big deal in the ag-
gregate, but it's made up of a bunch of little deals." He pointed to
a warehouse of less than 10,000 square feet across the parking lot.
The effort caused the buttons on his shirt to gap open. "I'd need to
be convinced that a very senior guy was actually going to work on
them."

"Okay. Now tell me what you think of your broker also representing a competing project," Jack asked.

"That's a no-no. I understand it happens out here, but I don't
want a broker with conflicts."

"Follow me for a minute," Jack interrupted and walked back
across the parking lot, past their cars and out to the street. Stand-

ing on the curb Jack pointed down the street to a barren tract of about five acres. Heavy equipment leveled asphalt in the just completed street. Other than that the lot was unimproved. "Did you know Mike Grazlyn has a listing on that?"

"The Bancroft project?"

Jack could hear the surprise and disappointment in Dick's voice. "Yeah, if your eyes are good enough you can just make out his name under our logo on that big red and white sign on the corner. He's on it all right, but I'm not sure how competitive it's going to be. You can see the infrastructure isn't even finished." Jack turned to look at the man standing beside him. "Even if Bancroft does have the balls to actually build those things, it'll be next spring before they're done."

Thompson stepped off the curb and walked into the empty street and studied the vacant lot. A dust devil swirled toward him. Dick shielded his eyes with his forearm, turned and walked back to join Jack. "I'm sure that Mike Grazlyn wouldn't steer buyers to another project. He's not going to screw me. I'm not worried about that, Jack. But I am worried about my company's policy. It says no dice to conflict, and I'm not gonna buck it. I just can't have a broker who represents me working on the same type product right down the street."

"Okay, I hear you." Jack's kept his voice firm. "That settles it. The brokers representing ACRE will be Paul Jensen and his son, Brent. I know that you've been impressed with Mike Grazlyn, but the Jensens are a great team. Brent's a fine young broker. Aggressive. He chases those gazelles as hard as anyone. You're going to like him. And it won't hurt to have the old lion himself on your team."

"If that's your call," Thompson answered, "those are the guys I'll talk to."

They turned and walked back to their cars parked side by side.

Jack pulled a car key from his pocket. "I'm going on vacation for two weeks starting Saturday."

"Where are you off to, ol' buddy?"

"We're going to fly back to Chicago, rent a car and drive across country on old Route 66. You know," Jack said in a melodic, singsong voice. "'Flagstaff, Arizona. Don't forget Winona. Kingman, Barstow, San Bernardino'… It's mostly Interstate 40 now, but there are still places you can drive the old road."

"Sounds like fun."

"Lorna and I planned the trip before I took this job, so Miles agreed to allow me a little early vacation," Jack explained. "Can you hold off the presentation until I get back?"

"You bet," Thompson answered. "After putting you on the hot seat, I want to make sure you're there."

"Thanks. I'll enjoy the trip more knowing what's waiting when I return."

"Oh, one other thing," Thompson added. "We're going to need a property manager on the project. Not just someone to water the flowers and collect the rents. Someone I can rely on to help me make decisions. Any recommendations?"

Jack thought for a second. "You remember Pete Mastrionni?"

"Of course," Thompson's voice rose half an octave. "When you were my broker in LA, he was Armenquest's guy. His project was our major competition. We wrestled with him over every deal. Tough competitor."

"The Armenquest Company is out of the development business," Jack said.

"Isn't everyone?" Thompson chuckled.

"The firm's managed to survive by getting into the property management business," Jack explained. "They've transferred Pete out here." Jack turned and looked down Vineyard Avenue. "In fact, his office is straight down the street."

"That solves my problem." Thompson sounded excited. "Thanks! I'll give Pete a call. You have a good time on Route 66. I'll see you when you get back."

They shook hands and said good-bye. Thompson walked back

across the lot to complete his inspection, a large ring of keys jangling in his hand.

*   *   *

Miles' back was to the door. The back of his bald head glistened. He was bent over the keyboard on the credenza behind his desk. Playing solitaire.

"Practicing your click and drag technique, I see," Jack said as he entered the office.

Miles finished dragging the three of hearts and releasing it onto the deuce at the top of the screen. He turned around in his chair and faced Jack.

Jack sat down. "Door was open so I let myself in."

"So I see," Miles responded as he opened his middle drawer and pulled out a letter opener. "What's on your mind?"

"National Commerce Bank," Jack answered.

"Have you decided?" Miles asked as he reached to the top of the stack of afternoon mail and plucked off a letter.

"The Jensens will represent us."

"I'm a bit surprised," Miles said without looking up from his task. "My sense was you were leaning toward Mike."

"Dick Thompson likes him a lot, but Mike has disqualified himself."

Miles looked up. "How so?"

"Mike represents Kevin Bancroft on a project that may be competitive to NCB's. Dick Thompson won't accept the conflict, and Mike won't give it up," Jack answered.

"So the Jensens win." Miles looked indifferent.

"Miles, I doubt Mike will come in and complain, but if he does...."

"I know," Miles held the palm of one hand up and toward Jack. "It's your call. We're agreed. The Jensens are ACRE's representatives on this one."

"Knock, knock."

Jack and Miles turned to the voice in the doorway.

"Sorry to interrupt," Irene apologized, "but I need your signature on my application for a real estate license." Irene, clearly pleased with herself, waved the official document at Miles.

"No problem, Irene. Jack and I were just finishing up," Miles said.

Jack rose to go. "One last thing, Miles. National Commerce Bank needed a property manager for the Cunningham project. I recommended Pete Mastrionni. I think Dick will hire him. That should merit a little appreciation from both of them."

"Can't hurt," Miles said. "When are you leaving?"

"This is it. I'm leaving now. Lorna and I fly out of LAX in the morning."

"Have fun." Miles looked directly at him with a smile. "Things will be in my hands while you're gone."

CHAPTER 11

Opportunity Knocks

"DO YOU always start this early in the morning?" Irene asked as she looked at Liz through slightly puffy eyes. "I don't mind getting up early, but five o'clock?"

Liz suppressed any expression of sympathy or understanding she might have felt. Training started now. "You want to stay on the switchboard, you can sleep in."

Irene tossed her dark curls as she straightened. "That's the last complaint you'll ever hear from me about schedule." Her smile faded into a look that chronicled her struggle to accept the rebuke with grace.

Never beat a compliant puppy, Liz thought. "That's better," she said as she lifted her own expression. "Irene, you and I can have a lot of fun together, but you can never forget we have to be better at this than they are."

"They?" Irene asked.

"It's a man's business we're in. A tough man's business at that. And every damn one of them believes he can toy with you. You can give-up, butch-up or control." Liz looked across the room toward the waitress. When she'd caught her eye, Liz made a gesture of pouring with one hand and held up two fingers of the other. The waitress nodded and shuffled toward the end of the counter where the coffee machine filled up its first pot. "Control gets you the most," Liz continued.

"Cream or sugar?" the waitress interrupted as she set two thick ceramic mugs on the table.

"Black," Liz responded without looking.

"Cream," Irene smiled at the sleepy-eyed waitress, who sauntered back to the counter.

Liz picked up her mug. She blew across the top, started to sip but placed it back on the table. "You play the feminine role only when it serves you, and you never let them use it against you. It's a game, and being a woman is a real good hand to be dealt once you learn how to play your cards."

"Ready?" the waitress asked as she slid the aluminum cream pitcher toward Irene.

"Pan sandwich, eggs easy and bacon crispy." Irene looked at Liz when she finished.

When the waitress' eyes reached her, Liz ordered. "Dry, sourdough toast."

"And sleeping is a weakness?" Irene asked, after the waitress left.

Liz pointed to the only other patrons in the place, a table of loud men dressed in jeans and T-shirts. One had a large leather wallet chained from his belt to his back pocket. "See them?"

"How could I miss them. When I walked in, they almost wouldn't let me by."

Liz smiled, tested her coffee again, and this time took a sip. "What do you figure their wives are doing right now?"

Irene stirred cream into her coffee. "Maybe trying to get breakfast for three kids and get them off to school?"

"Good enough. And what do you figure those guys think they're doing?"

"Sleeping in?"

"Exactly, it makes them feel superior to see us as weak. You buy into it for a second, and you'll never be their guy. And I'm not even talking about the ones that think a woman is nothing but a life support system for a pussy."

Irene blushed and then giggled. "Liz!"

Liz smiled. "It's true. There's one client I've done over a million feet of deals for, and his eyes still don't register dollar signs when he sees me. He sees me as a future fuck. Pete Mastrionni, what a piece of work."

Irene set down her fork. "Pete Mastrionni. Property manager?"

"He is now. Used to be a developer." Liz arched one eyebrow. "You know him?"

"Just heard Jack mention his name before he went on vacation. Jack recommended him as manager of an industrial park, I think."

"Which one?" Liz became very attentive.

"I'm not sure I heard." Irene dabbed her lips with the paper napkin. "No, I did—National Commerce Bank. That was it."

Liz relaxed. "NCB doesn't own anything out here to require management, Irene. Details like that can be important. You'll need to start remembering specifics." She took a sip from her cup.

Irene frowned as she looked across the room and seemed to focus on the big-rigs parked outside. "I'm pretty sure I remember that right." She continued to gaze outside. "Maybe there was a Cunningham in it somewhere."

"Jesus Christ," Liz exploded. A fine spray of coffee spewed from her mouth. "Jack referred Mastrionni to manage the Cunningham project for NCB? Is that what you're saying?"

Irene stared open-mouthed and said nothing for a moment. "Yeah, I guess that's it," she spoke haltingly. "Is something wrong?"

Liz recovered. "Nothing wrong. In fact there may be an opportunity here. Sounds like NCB foreclosed on Cunningham and my dear old client Pete Mastrionni is going to be the property manager. Maybe he needs a broker," she said.

"I think he already has one."

The smile fell from Liz's face as she focused on Irene again. She said nothing as she waited for Irene to continue.

"I was in Miles' office the day Jack left and heard him telling

Miles about Pete and NCB and Cunningham. Just as I walked in I heard Miles say, 'So the Jensens win.'"

Liz continued to focus on Irene. "So?"

"So, I think Jack assigned Paul and Brent to the account," Irene answered.

"Pan san." The waitress slid the plate toward Irene. "And dry sourdough." She put Liz's order down. "Anything else, girls?"

Liz looked up. "I'll take the check, dear," she said in a condescending tone.

Liz let a smile wash over her face as she picked up her knife and reached for the jam. "Maybe," she said. "We'll see...."

* * *

As Liz Peterson merged into the rush hour traffic on the San Bernardino Freeway she let her mind wander back over her career. She graduated cum laude from the University of Southern California School of Business in 1980, and immediately sought and gained a training position with American Corporate Real Estate Company. Liz wanted money. And she wanted it now! No slow crawl up some corporate ladder with a glass ceiling at the top for this girl.

And no relying on some man to get it for her either. She'd seen her mom, the supportive little wifey, do that. And she'd seen her get dumped by Dad when she'd dried up. Yeah, she got alimony and the house, but she was washed up. Dad was on top of the world. A company to run, games to play and a pretty young thing to sleep with.

That old jazz singer said it all, "God bless the child that's got her own." She planned to make sure it was "her own," and not someone else's—someone who could take it away any time.

And what faster way to get her own than commissioned sales on big-ticket items? And what was a bigger ticket item than a warehouse? There might not be the glamour of representing high fashion retailers along Montana or Melrose, but there was more money—a lot more money—in industrial property. If she had to spend her days with potbellied, cigar-smoking men who ran trucking companies and cold rolled steel businesses, so be it. Daddy'd taught her how to handle them. And if she had to spend her nights learning about rail sidings, and truss heights, and blind-side backing, and fire sprinkler calculations, she could handle that too. All she wanted was the big payoff.

For training, Liz had been assigned as a "runner" for a moderately successful industrial specialist, Paul Jensen. No one remembered a better runner. She would do anything, go anywhere, meet anyone to make a deal. During her year of training, Paul made more money than in any of his previous fifteen. At the end of the year, Paul invited Liz to become his partner.

It was an extraordinary offer, and Liz knew it. She also knew that the talk on the street was that she fucked her way into the partnership. Well, fuck them.

They made a good pair. He had contacts and charisma. She drove hard and didn't miss details. And it worked. In each of the ten years of their partnership, they made more money than they had the previous year—even during the last two years, the period when Paul had spent half his time playing cowboy in New Mexico and the other half fishing. He'd stop in on his way through LA and come to a meeting or two and play big man. The rest of the time she'd cover for him. Cover with clients, management and other brokers.

And she begged! Her, Liz Peterson. She had begged Paul to come back to work. If he wasn't going to come back, then he should retire.

Paul just laughed. He'd told her to see it as a chance to grow—to see if she could do it without him in the lead. Besides, he'd gotten her started. It was her turn to take care of him for awhile.

Well fuck that! The free ride's over. Mr. Paul Jensen and I are no longer partners, and best as I can figure, he owes me over a million dollars I gave him while he was fishing and playing cowboy. It's payback time!

*　*　*

Pete Mastrionni stood at his window peering into the parking lot three stories below. She'd said four o'clock, and it was ten 'til. She'd be here soon, he thought, just as the white Lexus pulled in. Pete watched the big sedan slide into one of the vacant guest stalls directly below. When the door opened his patience was rewarded by the sight of her long legs swinging out and presenting themselves in disembodied glory. She is sexy for a cold bitch, he mused. And always interesting. It will be fun to see what she wants now.

Pete turned from the window and viewed his modest office. He'd never thought it would be like this. When he'd completed his MBA at Stanford, Pete knew exactly what he'd wanted. He wanted to get wealthy. And, he knew how to do it, too. The big money was in commercial real estate development. Where else could you use somebody else's millions, have them pay you a fee for taking a risk with their dough and make you a partner? It was too good to be true.

But Pete also knew that banks and other institutions didn't make those deals with just anybody. But there was a system in place to get them. Pete just had to hook on as a leasing agent with some large commercial developer and work his way up. With a lot of hard work, a little luck and a few successes, Pete could make himself an instrument of the firm's expansion. He'd put deals together and get some of the ownership—equity in the property.

Equity! That's how you got wealthy. Somebody else supplied the debt and you "created" the equity. Equity you could sell for real dollars.

Well, it was a great scheme. He had made all the right moves —gone to the right schools, gotten on with The Armenquest Company and worked his ass off. If Pete had been forty-two instead of thirty-two, it would have worked. He'd have made his money and gotten out before it all collapsed. How the hell could he have known that the equities game was going to die with the 'eighties?

And now he found himself like every other developer on the West Coast—scrambling for jobs just to stay afloat. Consultation, asset management, property management, call it what you will, it all amounted to the same thing. He had to sell his knowledge and skills for fees instead of equity positions. He remained an employee instead of an owner.

Dick Thompson had offered him a job as a property manager. Christ! He and Dick had started their careers with competing projects in Los Angeles. Now he worked for Dick. Christ!

Well, it wouldn't do any good to bitch and moan. He needed the contract and the first step toward collecting the bonus at the end of the assignment would be to assist Dick in picking a broker.

Generally, that was an easy enough job, but it looked like it was going to be a little dicey with ACRE. Dick had told him that Jack Kendrick had named the brokerage team from ACRE—Paul and Brent Jensen.

Shit, Pete thought. He really didn't look forward to this.

Paul Jensen had been doing business with T.T. Armenquest since the beginning. But about all T.T. did anymore was take French and piano lessons. And Paul spent most of his time branding cows the old-fashioned way with branding irons and a wood fire. Christ.

Now Pete was going to have to listen to Paul Jensen philosophize about the market, do damn little work and show up every now and again to act like a living legend. And Brent Jensen. Paul's toady. What an arrogant prick. He figured the way to become as successful as his father was to be as cocky.

He'd sure hoped for more than this.

*   *   *

"Pete's expecting me," Liz handed her card to the pretty, young woman behind the reception desk.

"I'll tell him you're here," the blond responded

Liz watched as she rose from her desk and walked across the reception area to Pete's private office. The rigidity of her big breasts under the tight sweater gave mute evidence of a boob job. Bet he's boffing the little bitch.

A moment after the receptionist disappeared into his office, Pete appeared. "Liz, lovely as always," he greeted her.

"Flattery will get you everywhere, you suave, good-lookin' devil," she responded.

Liz looked at the man standing on the other side of the waiting room, arms flung open to her. He was of medium height with deep, close-set eyes. His wavy brown hair was combed straight back with the receding sides creating an exaggerated widow's peak, the point of which divided his face into sharp plains. His hawklike nose heightened the effect.

As he approached, Liz grasped both Pete's thin shoulders firmly and held him slightly at bay as she kissed the air next to his ear.

After they separated he pointed to his open door. "Come in. I'm interested to hear what's on your mind." As they passed the exiting receptionist, he added, "Cryptic references to mutual opportunities from gorgeous brokers always excite me."

She took the leather padded armchair in front of Pete's desk and looked for a moment out the window behind him. She should have been able to see all the way up Vineyard Avenue to the San Gabriel Mountains. But this was July and late in the afternoon. Everything the South Coast Air Quality Management District tried to control but couldn't was stacked right up against them. She couldn't see half a mile. But she could see the grin on Pete's face.

"Well?" he asked.

She slowly crossed her knees and smoothed the hem of her skirt. "It appears congratulations are in order."

Pete sat with his hands gripped around the front of the chair arms.

"I understand you're managing the old Cunningham project for NCB."

Pete smiled slowly. "News travels fast."

"Only to those who know how to interpret it," she said. "How'd you get it?"

Pete looked at her for a moment, and then shrugged. "Years ago, I competed for tenants with a US Equities project. A fellow by the name of Dick Thompson ran it. He's now with NCB."

At the mention of NCB, Liz's blue eyes started to twinkle. "And?" she prodded.

"NCB has just taken the property back, as you appear to know. And, Dick called a few days ago and asked me to manage it." Pete swiveled his chair around and pointed out the window, up Vineyard toward the project. "Some two dozen small buildings for sale." He swiveled back. "They've been vacant for a while, but there's nothing wrong with them that some aggressive marketing won't cure."

"Cunningham's been trying to sell them for enough money to cover his loan." Liz's tone was skeptical. "The market's well below that."

"Now that the bank has them back, they'll write down the loan, and sell them at whatever number it takes to get them off the books."

"You're going to need a broker."

"Yeah. One of my first directives was to call the main brokerage houses and set up listing presentations," Pete said.

Liz leaned back, uncrossed her long legs and smiled. "Okay, when do you want a listing presentation?"

Pete frowned. It was a puzzled frown. "Liz, you'd be my pick to work this, but it's a little more complicated than that."

"What could be complicated? You want me, you got me."

Pete let his eyes drift down her body, and a smirk slowly formed on his face. "There's a problem," he said. "Dick Thompson asked Jack Kendrick to pick ACRE's representative. Jack designated Paul and Brent Jensen."

Liz sat upright. "Jensen? He's not going to work that stuff. And you don't even like him."

"Now, Liz, I don't dislike Paul Jensen," he chided.

She leaned well forward in her chair, but her tone calmed. "All right, Pete, you're on the record. You don't dislike Paul Jensen. But he sure as hell's not going to work these little buildings, and his kid couldn't identify a hot prospect if one stood in front of him and waved cash."

"Liz, even if I agreed with all that," Pete said as the worry lines reappeared on his forehead, "I've got specific directions from Dick. I don't think it's a good idea to start by ignoring one of his directives."

"Look, Pete, if the problem is that Jack has designated another team, I'll take care of it," Liz said in a very flat tone.

"No," Pete shook his head, "I'll talk to Jack. Why don't you have him call me?"

Liz leaned forward in her chair. "Pete, Jack's out of town. I'll take care of it. I promise you it will be fine."

Again the skin wrinkled on his high forehead. "Liz, I'm not going to stick my neck out that far for you."

Liz unbuttoned her jacket and stood. Her arms fell to her sides, her nipples almost visible through the sheer fabric of her blouse. "What are you willing to stick out for me?"

Liz watched as Pete rose and came around the desk toward her. He stopped directly in front of her and stood toe to toe, inches from her. "Like I said," she purred, "you want me, you got me."

"I've been waiting for years for that offer," he said.

She could feel his hips and belly pressed into her as Pete put his arms around her. His breath warmed her face as she rubbed her breasts into him.

She knew what little control he had left would be gone in seconds. She'd be in complete control, and he'd do whatever she asked. The thought thrilled her far more than his embrace.

When he placed his lips on hers, Liz moved neither to him nor away. This was the critical moment. She'd hold out hope enough for lust to cloud his judgment, and keep control so she could manipulate Pete's weakness. Liz held her body neither rigid nor submissive as she felt his hands glide down her back and onto her ass. Again she placed her hands on his shoulders and slowly pushed until she felt him come to a stop against the desk. When his face was far enough away for her to focus, Liz indulged an enigmatic, almost sardonic, smile.

He let go.

"This will amount to a couple of million in commission," she said. "For a contract that big, you deserve a lot better than this."

"This is what I want." He put his hands on her shoulders and turned her toward the couch behind her. "Right here, right now," he panted.

Liz stepped away and around the chair, turned and fixed Pete with a stern look that froze him completely.

He took a step back, leaned his hip on the front of his desk and looked at her.

Liz softened her expression. "I've just employed a new assistant," she spoke barely above a whisper. "She's nineteen, gorgeous, and has tits so big that when you get in there you won't be able to hear a thing." She gave Pete a knowing grin. "It's time to bring her further into the business." Liz towered over his half-sitting figure. She looked down at his swollen erection outlined against the rich brown fabric of his trousers. "We'll need to have dinner and celebrate. We'll be working together for a long time and the team members need to get to know each other intimately. The night you deliver a listing contract, I'll deliver Irene." Liz turned to leave.

As she crossed the office Liz felt his eyes watching her move. She placed her hand on the doorknob, stopped and looked over her shoulder. "You never know what might happen at a celebration."

*   *   *

Liz had been at her cube for three hours when Miles strolled in around nine-thirty. She gave him time to down a cup of coffee and read the morning mail. When she saw that nobody else was in his office, she walked over and knocked on Miles' open door.

Liz smiled sweetly. "Hi, Miles. I've got some good news for my favorite manager."

Miles ignored the knock momentarily, and then looked up. He returned Liz's smile and pointed to one of the two chairs in front of his desk. "We could use a little good news around here."

"Actually," Liz said as she folded into the chair, "it couldn't be much better. We're about to get a listing on twenty-five free-standing buildings that are priced right."

Miles reached for the top item on the stack of morning mail, ripped the envelope open and pulled out a preprinted brochure. He gazed at Liz over the top of the flyer. "If they're priced right, I presume you're listing them from the lender. What project is it? Who took it back?"

Liz kept her smile in place. "I'm taking the listing from the property manager. NCB got the Cunningham project back and then gave the property management to Armenquest. Pete Mastrionni's asked me to make a presentation. It's just a formality though. I'll get the listing."

Miles shuffled through a stack of documents. "National Commerce Bank? Isn't that the project that Jack assigned to Paul Jensen?"

"That's the project but it's not the same deal. Paul's been going after NCB directly through his relationship with Patch Patterson. But now NCB's out of the loop and Pete's going to make the decision. Frankly, Miles, Pete told me that if we came at him with Paul Jensen, we'd lose. By me, it's a new decision-maker and a new deal. I just wanted to make sure you knew."

Miles looked up from the stack of papers he thumbed through. "Pete has control now?"

Liz nodded solemnly.

"And Pete won't give the listing to Paul?"

"Pete feels Paul's not going to work on the project, and that his son is too weak to work it without him," she answered.

"Okay, Liz, sounds like a new deal to me and it sounds like you're in charge," Miles said. "Be sure to tell Jack when he gets back."

"Will do," she said. "One other thing. I'm going to need Irene. You promised her to me when the staff got through with their summer vacations."

"When do you need her?"

"I'll need her full time once we get the listing signed and the marketing effort starts. Before that, all I need is a few hours to help prepare a presentation."

"I'll get it scheduled to get her off the board when you need her," he said. "Let Irene know, would you?"

"I'll go talk to her now," Liz said, and then she smiled at him. "I knew there was a reason you were my favorite."

Liz was pleased with herself when she left Miles' office. It had been easy.

"Irene, get someone to take the board for a minute and come join me in the conference room," Liz directed.

"Be right there," came the cheery response.

Moments later Irene walked into the small conference room. The full skirt of her summer dress accentuated her grace. Its bright yellow color made her brown eyes luminous. "What's up?"

"Miles tells me I can't have you for a month," Liz answered. "But I need you now, so he's agreed to part time."

"Great. What can I do?"

"Your tip may work out." Liz lowered her voice. "We may get the listing."

"Really!" Irene squealed and jumped up and down. "Wow!"

Liz smiled at the enthusiastic display. "If we do, it will be a perfect opportunity for you to learn about marketing commercial property. Who knows where it may lead."

"Oh, my heart be still," Irene said with a smile that lit her entire face. "A future without a switchboard in it."

"You just do what I tell you, and you'll forget how to operate one of those things," Liz directed. "First, I'll need you to help me prepare the listing presentation. But, don't tell anyone what we're working on." Liz pointed through the glass wall of the conference room to the bullpen on the other side. "We're going to have to compete for this, and some of our competition is right out there."

"I'm not about to screw up before I even get started. My lips are sealed," Irene assured.

"Good. Incidentally, when the listing's signed, I'm going to take Pete out to dinner to celebrate. If you want, you can come along. We'll let our hair down a bit." Liz looked at Irene's long curls and allowed her gaze to follow them down to the hollow of her neck where they came to rest. "We'll all be working closely together for a long time. We might as well get to know each other on a personal level and have some fun."

"Fun I'm good at," Irene said and shook her shoulders to make her curls shake. The gesture also jiggled the top of her breasts showing above her square cut bodice.

Both women laughed.

"Pete will be an excellent contact for you. He's a powerful guy. And," Liz added with a conspiratorial smile, "it doesn't hurt a bit that he's cute."

CHAPTER 12

Route 66

OKLAHOMA divides the hills of Missouri from the hardpan plains of West Texas, and its terrain is a blend of both. Oklahoma's hills roll much more gently and slowly than the craggy limestone buttresses of Missouri. But it is not nearly so bland, flat and featureless as the ancient seabed of the Texas Panhandle. Jack and Lorna drove along these hills following the setting sun. Its rays filtered through low clouds trailing a summer squall and cast a soft light that covered the earth in warm tones of gold and red and painted slowly lengthening purple shadows.

Lorna's head had been lying against the passenger's side window. She rolled it slowly toward him. "Tell," she commanded.

"Tell what?"

"You haven't spoken in an hour, so tell."

"Just thinkin'." He kept his eyes on the road.

"You still at work?"

"Sorry." He glanced over and gave her a quick self-deprecating smile.

"That thing with Thompson still worrying you?" she frowned.

His expression lifted as he turned to look at her. "You're right. I can't keep them on course from Oklahoma, now can I. They'll just have to do their best without me." He paused. "You hungry?"

"I'm not sure how hungry I am, but my butt's getting tired of sitting. "

Jack again took his eyes from the road and looked at his wife. This time a devilish grin turned up the crow's feet at the corners of his eyes.

Lorna brought her head up straight and looked stern. "Don't say a word about my bony ass. Not one word."

Jack's expression didn't change. "Yes, dear." He looked back at the road. "I am starting to get hungry. Joplin was the last time we stopped. How about you and your bony..."

"I warned you," Lorna interrupted.

Jack still smiled as he finished his statement. "How about you," he paused, "start contemplating some place we can stop. 'Cause if you leave it to me, I'm apt to pull into a McDonald's and then you'll be mad at me for two hours."

Lorna squeezed all the skin on her face toward her eyes in an expression of disgust, "Yuck. I can do better than that. I'm sure I can find us a nice kitschy local Oklahoma cafe that serves chicken fried steak and mashed potatoes, that are actually mashed, with brown gravy over the whole thing."

She sat up in her seat and peered through the windshield. "Like that." She pointed at a big yellow billboard at the top of the hill. "Buffalo burgers, the sign says they sell buffalo burgers at this joint," Lorna giggled with glee. "St. Cloud Exit, only two miles. That's our stop."

He didn't see any activity along the farm-to-market road that proceeded from the tollbooth. But they were reassured by the appearance of another big yellow billboard.

"Only one mile on the left," Lorna said.

Jack was peering intently on the left-hand side of the road. "There it is. Just where they said it would be. Only it looks closed."

He turned off the two-lane asphalt into a gravel parking lot that could've held a couple of hundred cars. A row of low wooden buildings spread out before them, but not a light showed anywhere. Jack parked in front of what appeared to be the main building. Theirs was the only car in the lot.

He got out of the car, walked around and opened Lorna's door. When she stepped out he wrapped his arms around her. She bent backwards over his arms in an exaggerated arch. "Oh, it feels good to stretch," she said.

"I think we're a little late for buffalo burgers, but this place is fascinating. Let's take a look," Jack said, as he took his arms from around his wife.

The building immediately in front of them was a wood-framed structure fronted by a long, covered porch. A sign on the roof read "Buffalo Ranch." Three wide board steps led up from the graveled lot. A porch swing, suspended on chains, swayed slowly. The building to the right was a close mate to the one in front except that the sign on the roof read "Buffalo Cafe." In smaller print underneath it offered "Buffalo Steaks and Burgers." Another long, low structure stood to their left. It had no sides and covered an enlarged wheel laid horizontal to the ground. The spokes extended about fifteen feet from its hub and hung three feet off the ground. Jack guessed it to be a pony ride of some sort.

Even more interesting than the odd assortment of buildings were the birds. On the swing, the low eaves of the porch and an old fashioned hitching post in front, birds were beginning to roost for the evening. They were beautiful and exotic species. Their lack of confinement and the ubiquitous droppings added to the unkempt appearance of the place.

The only birds not roosting were a pair of brown geese in the middle of the parking lot. One stood oddly close behind the other, and they both flapped their wings frantically.

Jack put both hands on Lorna's shoulders and turned her until she faced the pair. "I do believe they're doing it, my darling."

Lorna smiled. "Lucky little gander, isn't he?"

"Lucky?" Jack sounded surprised. "He's probably slaved all day long looking around this stony parking lot for little pieces of grain for her, and he may even have found a sprig or two of fresh grass.

Lucky indeed. He's no doubt been a responsible and devoted mate who's only accepting the attention he richly deserves."

"Oh, vacations do relax you, don't they?" Lorna teased as she grabbed his hand and turned toward the pony ride. "Let's see what else this place has to offer."

Behind the pony ride, Jack saw a series of whitewashed animal pens. In the flat evening light he could make out a green pasture behind them. The pasture rolled gently downhill toward a wood lot.

"Been on the road awhile?" The soft voice from behind startled Jack. As he turned to face the speaker, he wondered that he hadn't heard the approach of the tall, thin man with windblown, sandy hair. The man wore an old pair of jeans and boots and a clean but rumpled khaki shirt with a collar and long sleeves buttoned up against the cooling evening. As Jack's original surprise left him, he thought that this man looked very much like a down-on-his-luck Gary Cooper.

"Sorry to disappoint you folks, but it's Monday. Buffalo Ranch is closed today."

"Shucks. We've been following your big yellow signs for two hundred miles," Lorna said. "I was really looking forward to my first Buffalo Burger."

"There's no way to open the kitchen," the cowboy apologized with a soft smile. "But if you're interested, I can show you around. Give you the nickel tour." He walked past them toward the animal pens.

Jack and Lorna looked at each other. Lorna nodded and Jack shrugged. They followed the receding figure. When he got to the pens, the middle-aged roustabout raised a loop of rope connecting the gatepost to the fence and swung the gate open. "Close it behind you," he said as he proceeded down an aisle between rows of pens. He stopped at a corral full of ponies.

A deer, not more than three-and-a-half feet at the shoulder

with a rack of antlers disproportionately large for its little body, was darting about at the back of the pen. Jack half expected to see it fall forward onto its face. The little buck ran four or five steps, jumped quickly to its left and butted one of the ponies with its huge rack.

"Slips in here about this time every day. Jumps one of them low fences at the back." The wrangler pointed toward the pasture. "He don't want nothing but to play with the ponies. He's got the same salt and grain out there, they've got here. And out there he's got a bunch of does. But he likes to come in here and torment these ponies 'cause he's quicker 'n they are. Ain't he rich?"

Lorna and Jack smiled, as much at the roustabout's question, as at the little buck's playful antics.

"Ever seen a baby buffalo up right close?" he asked as he slowly walked toward another pen. Jack looked through the iron stanchions and saw a great shaggy buffalo standing at a hay feeder, looking as calm and domestic as a Holstein cow.

"Come on over here. You can see her baby."

Lorna drew near the fence, and pointed at the little calf. "Ah, look honey. Look at those eyes. So big."

As she said it, the wrangler stuck a hand through the bars and the little buffalo lowered its head and walked right into his outstretched palm. He scratched the calf between its budding horns. "Cute, ain't he?"

As they stood talking in the gathering dark, Jack noticed one of the ponies looked different than the others. In fact, it looked like a mule, but pony-sized. "What kind of animal is that?"

"Well," came the drawling response, "you know what a mule is. It's just a cross between a burro and a horse. In this case, I guess someone crossed a burro with a pony. He's so funny lookin'; I bought him for a friend of mine 'cause I thought he'd get a bang outta him. See how ropy the muscles in his neck are? Comes from a disease called withers. Makes them pretty much useless. He was in an auction. If I wouldn't a bought him, he'd a ended up dog food. I only paid twenty-two dollars for him, and I give him to my pal on his birthday. He kept him for about six months, but the damn little mule did nothin' but kick his cows, and he had to get rid of him. I was working here by then, so I just put him in the pen here with these ponies." He paused. "Where are you folks from anyway?"

"Los Angeles," Jack said.

"California, huh? I was there wonst," the wrangler said. "On my way back from Viet Nam. Got discharged at Camp Pendleton and jus' went on up to LA."

"So how'd LA treat you?" Jack asked.

"Big city," the cowboy said with a pensive smile. "Whole lot of temptations for a country boy. Too many things to resist. After a couple of years, I drifted back here where it's easier for a man to do right."

By now, the only things clearly visible in the gloom were the whitewashed metal stanchions. They started back down the alley between the pens.

"What do you do here?" Jack asked.

"I'm the watchman at night, and I run the pony rides in the day. It's a livin'. The old couple that owns this place, he's seventy-one and she's seventy. There's a lot they could do to make it better, but there's just no one that's got interest. I help out how I can. They give me a room and half the take from the pony ride."

They walked through the last gate and the wrangler closed it and laid the rope loop back over the post.

"Thanks for the tour," Jack said as he extended his hand.

The wrangler looked at the hand and the five-dollar bill Jack palmed there. "You're sure welcome, but you can put that bill back in your pocket. I showed you around 'cause I thought you'd enjoy it. No other reason."

Jack waited a moment, but when the wrangler made no move to take his hand, he put the bill away. "Thanks. We did enjoy it."

"Glad ya did." He paused. "You folks are the second bunch

I've shown around today. Earlier a van full of kids—black kids—from Tulsa stopped by. They were hanging around the ride and asked when it was gonna open. I tol' 'em we was closed for the day, but one of the little 'uns said, 'Ah, mister we're from Tulsa and we've never been on ponies before. Please?' So I went out and got four of the ponies and got 'em in harness and tol' the kids it was a dollar a ride. They said they didn't have that much, so I let them all get on the ponies and ride. They musta' took twenty rides. When they left, the lady drivin' the van, give me five dollars and said thanks." The aging cowboy's face was serene. "Well, they'd never had a pony ride before."

By now, they were standing in the parking lot. Jack pointed at the well-lit cinder block building on the other side of the road. "Is the food any good in the cafe?"

Lorna spoke up before the cowboy could answer. "Do they serve buffalo burgers?"

The tall cowboy shook his head slowly. "Nope, we're the only ones around with buffalo burgers, and we're only open for lunch. But their food's just fine."

Jack extended his hand toward the cowboy. "I'm Jack and this is my wife, Lorna."

The cowboy gripped Jack's hand and nodded toward Lorna. "My name's John."

"Well, John, Lorna and I are going to have dinner so let's say good-bye now. We sure appreciated your tour. Thank you."

"It was my pleasure," John said as he released Jack's hand. "If you're ever back here again, stop in and say Hi. I'll be here." And then he nodded his head toward Lorna. "Pleased to meet you ma'am."

Jack and Lorna turned and walked toward the two-lane asphalt road and the cafe on the other side. Lorna reached up and put her arm around Jack's shoulders. She leaned into him far enough to grab the biceps on his far arm. "What ya thinkin'?" she asked.

"About the aging Gary Cooper," Jack answered.

Lorna laughed. "John? Yeah, that pretty well describes him. What are you thinking about him?"

"Well…" Jack stopped to let an eighteen-wheeled truck that was outfitted as a double-decked cattle car pass before he and Lorna crossed to the gravel parking lot of the cafe. "It's not so much him I'm thinking about as fate…kismet."

Lorna just looked at him and held tight to his arm as they crossed the road.

Jack continued, "You know, I grew up not far from here. What if my folks hadn't moved to LA?"

Lorna looked at him quizzically. "What's that got to do with our Gary Cooper?"

They stepped between a new Chevrolet Caprice, painted and decaled in the distinctive black and white style of almost every police jurisdiction in the country, and a five-year-old Ford half-ton truck whose bed was fitted with high wooden sides used for hauling big animals. "He could be me," Jack said.

They walked the few remaining steps to the cafe door, where Lorna stopped to allow Jack to open it for her. She stepped through and then looked up at Jack. "You're such a drama king. He's nothing like you." She entered.

The cafe was a large hall with a counter that extended the length of the room. The kitchen was behind the counter with an aluminum order wheel and a bell for the cook to ring as he announced to the entire room, "Order up!" The other three walls were lined with red naugahyde-covered booths. A few square tables set on single center posts were randomly placed in the open space in the center of the room.

"Perfect!" Jack said, more to himself than Lorna.

They seated themselves in a vacant booth next to the deputy whose car was parked outside. He was holding forth that the trouble with the Oklahoma football program was the NCAA. The NCAA had set out to ruin every football powerhouse. Except

Notre Dame. Even the NCAA was afraid to mess with Notre Dame.

The waitress strode purposefully toward them. Her hair was pulled into a bun from which a yellow pencil extended over her right ear. She clutched a coffeepot in one hand and menus in the other.

"Coffee, yawl?"

"Thanks, black," Jack answered up with a smile.

"Do you really mash the potatoes?"

"No, honey, the cook does. I just serve 'em." She poured Jack's coffee and looked down at Lorna with a self-satisfied, and half-combative, smile.

"Chicken-fried steak and mashed potatoes," Lorna announced. "Don't need the menu."

Jack got a cheeseburger and fries.

After their dinner arrived, Jack looked across at his wife. "You know you're wrong about John and me. We're very much alike."

"You're serious. Tell me," she said.

"John and I are both about fifty. We both started life with Viet Nam as our graduation trip."

"You and half a million other guys. So what?"

Jack stared at her.

"Okay, okay. I won't interrupt."

"Who knows what John did after he came back home? But whatever it was, you can bet he had no idea he'd end up at fifty living in a tack room and giving pony rides."

"So?" she asked.

"So I've been luckier than John. And about that you're right, we're different. But whatever it was that got John here, he's accepted it. All he's trying to do is find a place where he fits. And he's trying to make some right choices. Share some of the beauty of his world with a couple of strangers like you and me, or a van full of inner city kids who have never had a pony ride. And if those decisions don't serve his immediate self-interest—so be it. He's trying to do what's right. And in that, honey, John's just like me. He's struggling for the same things I am."

"More coffee, folks?" the waitress interrupted. "I see you liked our taters," she nodded to Lorna's almost empty plate.

Lorna smile up at her. "What's not to like? They're great. And, yes thank you, I will take a warm-up."

She refilled Lorna's cup and looked at Jack. He nodded and she refilled his. "Anything else? We've got some fresh berry pie."

"Stuffed."

"Me, too."

"Okay, I'll bring your check." She walked to the cash register.

Lorna blew across the top of her coffee cup. "I wish she'd pull her hair into a bun and carry a pencil stuck through it."

"The place is almost perfect, isn't it?"

Lorna's expression changed from delighted to sober. "Honey, if you and John are so much alike, and all you want is…" she paused, "a place to fit and to make some right choices." She paused again. "Then why don't you do what he did and go somewhere that it's easy to do?"

"Like move to Bozeman where I can pump gas and you can wait tables," Jack teased.

"If that's what's going to make life the way you want it, why not?"

"For one thing it gets down to twenty below in Bozeman."

Lorna didn't smile. She just stared at him over the top of her cup.

He looked down at his plate and picked up a french fry, then set it back down. "John and I are different in one big way." He looked up at her. "Remember why he said he left LA?"

"Yeah. Too many temptations. Too many things to resist. Something like that."

"Exactly." Jack moved his plate to one side and leaned across the table. "I can't do that, Lorna. The only way I can really succeed is to stay where I am. Where the consequences about choices are

big. And make some right decisions anyway. By me, that's a successful life." He stared into her brown eyes. "So am I still a drama
king?" he asked.

Lorna wiped up the last bit of gravy with her biscuit, popped
it into her mouth and finished her coffee. Only then did she smile
very sweetly at her husband. "I'm kinda glad you don't want John's
life as a lone wolf. As long as you want to run with the pack in LA,
I like living at the beach." She stood up, walked over to his side of
the booth, and sat down beside him. She put her hands on either
side of his face. "And yeah, you're still a drama king, but I love
you—very much."

CHAPTER 13

Welcome Back

LIZ ALWAYS made him nervous when she approached with that smile on her face. He couldn't figure out how on earth he could be intimidated by a woman four inches shorter and fifty pounds lighter than he was; but those realities didn't keep the adrenaline from pumping when she walked into his office with that smile—the one that said she wanted something. Not that Liz didn't always want something. As Lorna had pointed out, Liz had a million-dollar income and long legs. What the hell more could any woman want? But Liz wanted more and she was coming to get it.

At least, Jack thought, I won't have to wait long to find out. You never have to wait long with Liz.

"Did you have a nice vacation?" Liz asked with that smile still frozen in place.

"Nice enough that I've come to work very calm this morning," Jack answered. "But check with me tomorrow. By then I'll be back to my usual frantic self and won't even remember I had a vacation."

"Did you hear the good news?" she asked.

Here it comes.

"Pete Mastrionni is managing the Cunningham project," Liz continued, "and I'll be doing a presentation to get the listing. Actually we've already got the listing. The presentation's just a formality."

Jack struggled to keep his face from registering the shock. He leaned forward and reached for his coffee cup to buy a moment. He wasn't surprised that Pete was managing the project, but how the hell did Liz schedule a presentation? What had happened to Jensen and Jensen? Did Miles know this? So many questions, but he asked none of them. "Well, I'm not surprised Pete's managing the project because I recommended him to Dick before I left, but how are you involved?"

"I'm Pete's favorite broker." The frozen smile changed to show just a bit of self-satisfaction.

"What about Jensen? He was making the presentation when I left." Jack struggled to keep his voice flat.

Liz crossed her legs and pushed her jacket sleeves up her forearms. "Paul was trying to get the listing when National Commerce Bank was controlling it, but Pete's controlling it now. Pete told me that if Paul made the presentation, we'd never get the listing. Pete is the decision-maker now; it's going to be up to him. New decision-maker, new deal."

Liz uncrossed her legs and stood up from the chair. "Miles knows all about it. Check with him." She took one step toward the door and then stopped as though forgetting something and turned around. "Welcome back," she said, turned again and departed.

Jack didn't know what happened during his vacation, but he knew it wasn't going to take until tomorrow before he'd feel like he'd never been gone. Finding out started with Dick Thompson. But, Dick wasn't in, so Jack left a message that he needed to catch up. Then he got up and walked across the office.

Miles spent ten minutes asking about his cross-country drive before Jack could bring up the subject.

"Has something changed with the Cunningham/NCB Project?" Jack asked in a conversational tone. "Liz was in my office earlier this morning and said she'd arranged to make a presentation."

Miles' baldhead glistened, but his face showed only indifference. "I'm not exactly sure. Liz tells me that Armenquest has taken over management of the property and that Pete Mastrionni is picking the brokerage team. She also said that Pete told her that if we stayed with Jensen we'd lose the business. So, Liz is making the presentation."

Jack struggled to maintain his composure. "You authorized the change?"

Miles looked genuinely perplexed. "Well, it wasn't a case of authorizing anything. The decision-maker has changed and Liz is in front of the new one."

Jack exhaled, and instantly resigned himself to what he knew to be the obvious. His boss had managed, once again, to get out-positioned by a very aggressive sales person. Worst of all, Miles either didn't see it or didn't care.

His job wouldn't be made more pleasant or secure by pointing out to his boss that he was an incompetent fuck-up. Jack got to his feet. "Has anybody told Paul and Brent Jensen about this?"

Miles smiled pleasantly. "Not as far as I know. You might want to check on that though." Before Jack could respond Miles added, "Anyone tell you about Duran?"

"Duran?"

"Yeah, Jim Duran. My predecessor here."

"What about him?" Jack asked.

"He was rehired while you were on vacation."

"I thought he went into the development business. Didn't work out for him, huh?"

"Maybe not, but he's arranged a pretty soft landing," Miles said. "He's coming back to ACRE with a promotion."

Jack sat back down. "What job?"

"Duran will be the ramrod of the newly created Western Division." Miles looked down. "I'll be reporting to him."

Jack was perplexed. "New layer of management in tough times. Why?"

Miles shrugged but said nothing.

"You're no longer reporting straight to the president. What does that mean?"

"For now it means a seven-thirty breakfast meeting tomorrow at the Clarion Hotel. One of the first things Duran wants to do is to announce his triumphant return personally to his old office. Be there." Miles picked up the letter on top of his in-basket and ripped it open.

Jack rose to go.

"Oh, Jack."

He stopped and turned.

After a short pause Miles said, "I almost forgot. Welcome back."

Jack had almost finished cleaning up two weeks of mail when Dick Thompson called late in the day. Thompson started the conversation in his perpetual up-beat tone. "Hi, buddy. Welcome back. How was Route 66?"

After a few minutes of catching up, Jack got to the point. "I understand you've hired The Armenquest Company to do property management on the Cunningham Project."

"Yeah," Thompson said. "I appreciate your letting me know Pete had an office out by the project. I'm very comfortable with the guy. Nice to have an old competitor working for me. Oh by the way, we changed the name. It's now the Inland Industrial Park."

"Well, Dick, let me ask you the question that is nearest and dearest to my heart. Who's going to pick the broker for the Inland Industrial Park, you or Pete?"

"I have the authority, but the competitors are going to have to run the gauntlet between the two of us, ol' buddy."

"Okay, but has Pete said anything to you about changing the representative from ACRE?"

"Naw. I told Pete to set up the listing presentations, but I also told him that you would pick the team for ACRE, and that he should contact you. Why, is something wrong?"

Jack was choosing his words carefully now. "There's some talk

around here about people other than the Jensens making the presentation. I'm sure that Pete has some opinions. I'd like to talk to
him about it."

"Absolutely!" Thompson responded. "Call him and you two
select whatever individual or team is appropriate."

"Okay. I'll do that, right now." Jack was pleased for the opportunity to talk to Pete and find out how Liz had really gotten involved.

"You're not going to be able to get him today," Dick added. "I
think he's in San Francisco talking to some of Armenquest's lenders about extending one of their loans. Won't be back until tomorrow."

"All right. I'll call him early in the morning and get back to
you as soon as we've got it worked out."

Jack's phone rang the instant he hung up, a sure sign that Irene
had been keeping someone on hold until he was available.

"Bill Woodward here, Jack. I hear you've been on vacation.
Hope you had a good one."

Jack was silent, trying to recall who Bill Woodward might be.

"Deputy Bill Woodward. San Bernardino County Sheriff's
Department," the caller explained.

"Deputy. I'm sorry. Of course," Jack apologized. "How have
you been? And how did you know I'd been on vacation?"

"I called a couple of days after you left, and your office told me
you'd be gone for two weeks. I assumed the vacation part. Just calling because you asked me to when we finished the investigation on
the Montgomery Pierce case."

"Thanks, Deputy," Jack said. "I appreciate your calling. What
did you guys decide?"

"The coroner called it suicide."

"Suicide!" Jack was surprised. "Why'd he do it?"

"I can't say we found out."

"No note?" Jack leaned on his elbow, his ear propped against
the phone.

"We never found one."

"Then how'd the coroner decide it wasn't an accident?"

"Our investigation found no mechanical problem with Pierce's Celica," the deputy responded. "No failed brakes or steering or stuck throttle. And Pierce took no evasive action at all. It's as though he purposely aimed at the overpass support column."

"How do you know that?" Jack asked.

"The north and south bound lanes of the interstate are separated by a dirt median that's maybe twenty yards wide at that point," Deputy Woodward explained. "Pierce's tire tracks show he edged from the fast lane onto the median about four hundred yards before the point of impact. Headed straight for it."

"Is it possible he fell asleep or passed out with his hands locked to the wheel?"

"Not likely. Not there."

"What do you mean not there?" Jack pressed.

"The median is not only twenty yards wide, it's also five feet deep. Almost a ditch. At eighty miles per hour it would have taken a determined effort to hold the wheel straight when Pierce hit that dip. It was intentional all right," the deputy concluded.

"This is really hard to believe." Jack leaned on the phone in silence. He struggled to make some sense of it. "Was he drunk?" Jack finally asked.

"Drunk? By what standard?"

"Legally drunk," Jack snapped. "That standard."

There was a moment of silence before the deputy responded. "Pierce's blood alcohol was .08 percent. That's legally drunk in the Vehicle Code, just barely. But it wouldn't be enough to convict anyone of, say, public drunkenness. It sure isn't like he was out getting blind drunk. That's consistent with your Ms. Peterson's story."

"Liz?" Jack showed surprise. "What'd she know about his drinking?"

"You don't know?" the deputy asked.

"Know what?"

"Ms. Peterson and Montgomery and a customer of hers had dinner together that evening at the Ontario Hilton. They had wine with dinner. When she left, Montgomery and the client were getting along fine, and by her judgment not drunk at all, but she left early."

"Liz and Montgomery had dinner with a client?" Jack asked. "What client? Do you know?"

"Let see." There was the sound of paper rustling. "Here it is. Cornblatt. Oscar Cornblatt."

Jack sat in stunned silence. Liz and Montgomery and Cornblatt shared dinner and drinks. Liz left the client and a job candidate drinking together. Why would Liz do that? It wasn't like her to leave someone else in control when so much was at stake. And then Montgomery had driven into a freeway support column at eighty mph.

"Jack? You still there?" Deputy Woodward's voice brought him back.

"I'm here, Deputy. Sorry. This is all news to me," Jack answered. "How about the autopsy?"

"What about it?"

"Did the coroner just do a toxicology or the full on cut 'em open kind of autopsy?"

"Full thing. Needed to rule out heart attack, seizure—that sort of thing. Why?"

"Did it give any clue?" Jack asked.

"It's public record. I can send you a copy if you'd like."

"Yeah, well, okay. Go ahead, send it."

Jack cradled the receiver and pushed away from his desk. He reclined into his chair, closed his eyes and let his mind drift. He moved the pieces around to see what fit. Montgomery Pierce. Pretty and vulnerable. Would he really do anything to get the job? And Oscar Cornblatt. And Liz. How did they fit in, or did they? Only one way I know to find out.

Jack picked up the phone and dialed Liz's extension.

"Would you step into my office?"

A few minutes later she appeared.

"What's up?"

"I just got off the phone with the deputy who investigated the death of Montgomery Pierce."

"So what did they decide happened?"

"The coroner declared it suicide." Jack stared into Liz's eyes.

She hesitated a moment as a flicker Jack couldn't categorize crossed her face. Then control once again. "Suicide. Jesus, why'd he do that?"

"Liz, you didn't tell me that you took Montgomery to dinner with Oscar Cornblatt."

"You didn't ask." Liz's face became rigid and her chin thrust forward almost imperceptibly.

"No, I didn't ask. But I am now. Why did you take Montgomery to dinner with Cornblatt?"

"To interview him," she answered. "Remember, you asked me to."

"Over dinner?"

"Jack, it's done all the time." Liz was starting to sound exasperated. "As I recall, Miles interviewed you at the Turf Club," she added with a note of triumph.

"With a client? With Oscar Cornblatt?" Jack continued to question her.

"So what? So Cornblatt was there. What difference does that make?"

"You left them together, Liz? Why did you do that?" Jack persisted.

"God damn it, Jack. What is this all about? So I left them together. I left early. I've got a daughter who likes to see her mother every now and again. They were getting along famously, and I needed to go. What the hell do you care?"

"Liz, the autopsy report showed he was drunk."

"If he was drunk, Jack, it wasn't while I was picking up the tab," Liz assured him. "You needn't worry on that account."

Jack sat with his fingertips pressed together and stared at her.

"God damn it, Jack, we were sober. Ask the bartender," Liz protested.

"Yeah, like the Hilton is going to admit to serving drinks to an intoxicated patron who then goes out and kills himself," Jack spat. "But he got drunk. If not while you were buying, then maybe on Cornblatt's tab. I wonder what Vance Electronics would think about that?"

"What!" she screamed and bolted forward, her face showing fear for the first time. "Are you nuts? What are you going to do? Call Vance and accuse a very good customer of getting drunk with a young man who then kills himself? That won't do anything but ruin a good relationship with a huge client."

"No, Liz, you're right. I'm not going to call Vance. Not now." Jack locked his eyes onto hers.

Liz returned his stare, the muscles along her jaw clearly defined.

"You may go."

After she left, Jack stood and walked to the window. He stood at parade rest staring at the long shadows cast by the few cars remaining in the parking lot. Liz lost it for a moment. She got visibly upset when I threatened to call Vance. What's she scared of? Is it more than loosing the deal? There's something she's not saying. Did she let Pierce get drunk?

He had one more phone call to make before he could call it a day. He lifted the receiver and dialed Pete Mastrionni's number.

"You have reached the offices of Armenquest Property Services. Our office hours are from eight-thirty A.M. till five-thirty P.M. Please call back when someone is available or leave a message at the tone and we'll get back to you. *Beeeep*."

"Hi, Pete. Jack Kendrick here. I'd like to get hold of you to talk about the Cunningham...ah, check that, the Inland Industrial

Park presentation. Thompson tells me you're doing the property management and will be involved with him in selecting the brokerage company. I'd like to be certain you and I are on the same page about ACRE's representative in that competition. I've got a breakfast meeting tomorrow. I'll call you as soon as it's over."

                              *   *   *

The Stairmaster was demanding. Thighburner was more like it, Liz thought. It was the price a girl had to pay, and it did give her time to think. This evening she thought about Vance and Kendrick and Montgomery.

I can't believe the little bastard killed himself. Weaker even than I guessed. Well, the deal will still go fine. Vance is moving forward, and with a little luck they'll never know. If that deputy sheriff wanted to talk to Cornie he'd have done it before the coroner's finding, so that's not a problem. But Mr. "I Wonder What Vance Would Think?" Kendrick may be. What's he think, I killed the kid? Moralizing prick. This is business, not Sunday School. Even he's not stupid or self-righteous enough to poke around in it more than the coroner. Is he? Probably not. But that's a chance I don't think I'll take.

                              *   *   *

"Jim, forgive me for calling you at home. I just heard the good news."

"Liz Peterson, my star. To what do I owe this privilege?" Duran's raspy voice growled into the phone.

"You're back. I am so pleased," Liz purred.

"Well so am I. It's real hard to be a developer in a world full of empty buildings. So when I got the call to come home, promotion included…well, I'm here."

"And just in time, Jimmy," she said. "Things sure have gotten worse since my favorite manager left."

"I heard," Duran said. "The market sucks."

"Oh, for a smart girl who knows how to play her hand there's still money to be made."

"Even without Paul?" Duran asked.

Liz gave a little laugh. "Especially without Paul, big guy."

"Well then, what's so bad?"

"Mostly, my favorite manager isn't around making his usual brilliant decisions."

"Liz, don't kid me. You thought my decisions were brilliant because you benefited from most of them."

"And I never let you down," she reminded him. "It always came out the way you wanted."

"What's Miles Preston doing to piss you off, Lizzy?"

"Miles is okay. Him I can work with," Liz answered.

"The Sales Manager? Guy that got fired by So Cal Props. What's his name?" Duran guessed.

"Kendrick, Jack Kendrick. Quite a guy."

"Do I hear a little sarcasm?" Duran asked. "Tell me about him, Liz."

She did.

CHAPTER 14

Breakfast Meeting

AS JACK drove to the Clarion Hotel he mused about Jim Duran. He'd heard Duran's two distinguishing characteristics were his voice and his decisiveness. His voice, a high tenor, had so much grit and gravel in it that he perpetually sounded like he'd just taken a shot in the larynx with a two-by-four. His rather abrupt and forceful style was legendary. One of Duran's detractors had described it as, "Ready. Fire. Aim."

Most of the salesmen in Jack's office had worked for Duran. He was very popular with some, and disliked in the extreme by others.

When Jack arrived at the breakfast, he found the hotel ballroom had been divided until the nine rounds of eight needed to seat the entire staff were comfortably accommodated by its movable walls. Large, plastic chandeliers hanging from the high ceiling provided light. The contrast between the cheap but glitzy fixtures and the plain covering of the mobile partitions amused him.

A varnished wooden podium emblazoned with the hotel crest stood between two tables at the front of the room. This meeting was Miles' show. Jack wouldn't be involved so there was no reason for him to sit at the head table. He grabbed a cup of coffee from the service bar set up for early arrivals, went to one of the tables in the middle of the room and sat down. As the room started to fill, he noticed Liz's tall figure in the doorway. She surveyed the room, and upon seeing Jack walked straight toward him.

"May I join you?"

Jack felt a surge of adrenaline "Yeah, let's talk."

Liz pulled out a chair and sat down. She reached for the coffeepot and poured herself a cup.

"Let's discuss the Inland Industrial Park," Jack said.

"The what?" She looked over the top of her cup at him.

"NCB's changed the name of their project to the Inland Industrial Park," Jack explained. If she reacted in any way to his knowledge of the name change she didn't show it.

Liz blew over the top of her cup and set it down without drinking. "You talk with Miles?"

"Yeah."

She looked at him from over the rim as she blew again and then took a sip. "And?"

"Liz, this is my call. Always was." Jack studied her, but she didn't waver. "I've spoken to Dick Thompson as well as Miles. I'll talk to Pete Mastrionni and then decide whether it's you or the Jensens." Jack nodded a greeting in response to a "Hello" from across the room. "I'll get back to you then, Liz."

She set down her cup, rose and pushed back her chair. "Whatever you say, Jack." She smiled down almost benignly. "But you'll need to do it before three o'clock."

Jack snapped his head up to stare at her now smug smile. "Why three o'clock?"

"'Cause that's when I make the presentation." She stood up and left.

Just then, Miles tapped his water glass for attention and called the meeting to order. Jack barely heard Miles' introduction or Duran's initial address. All he could think of was how this had all gotten so out of control.

As he sat pondering, a question drove itself to the front of his mind. Miles doesn't care that Liz is taking the deal. Why the hell should I?

Duran's high, gravely voice droned on about challenge and contribution. Jack remained mired in his own thoughts. Is Liz Peterson a worse representative to NCB than the Jensens? Probably not. Then what the hell difference does it make? Why should I cause myself a lot of trouble over this? Why not just let it be? Shit, I've been gone two weeks and Miles changed personnel on the project. Not my problem.

It wouldn't wash and Jack knew it. If I let it slide, I'll give up what little authority I have with this bunch. Thompson told me to make the selection. If I can't make a decision when I'm asked to, they'll run right over me. My contribution is to manage this.

Jack suddenly felt better. Relieved. He knew what he had to do. He had to manage this.

When breakfast ended, he walked out of the meeting, got into his car and drove straight to Pete Mastrionni's office.

* * *

Decorum forced Jack to raise his eyes above her barely buttoned cashmere cardigan and to make eye contact. It was a struggle. "Is Pete in?"

"Is he expecting you?"

"Yes." Jack gave the half lie as he handed her his card. When she looked down to pick up the phone Jack's better instincts again struggled to avoid plumbing the depths of her sweater. This time they lost.

After a brief exchange on the phone, she again looked up. The slight look of disapproval said she'd caught him peeking. The eleven-year-old in his soul was embarrassed, even though the man knew it had been her intention to entice him.

"Pete asked if you could wait a few minutes for him to finish up a call."

"Of course."

"Can I offer you anything while you wait?" She paused. "A cup of coffee?"

"Thanks. Black."

As she crossed the room, Jack watched her ass move inside the defining confines of her too tight skirt. Bet Pete's boffing her.

After the receptionist brought him a cup of coffee, Jack strolled around looking at all the photographs and commemorative plaques in the waiting room. They depicted architectural and community awards for buildings Armenquest had constructed in the area. Before Jack finished viewing them, he heard Pete's voice behind him. "I'm glad you were able to stop in. I was looking forward to talking to you today."

Jack turned. Pete's thin frame was a clothes rack for the rich brown tropical worsted fabric of the Armani jacket. His face froze in a smile that evoked the image of a mortician trying to upgrade the widow from the plain pine coffin to the oak one with silver handles and a concrete liner. "Hello, Pete. Long time."

"Jack, the last time I saw you, you'd just stolen the Tecnocor deal, and taken them to Thompson's project."

Despite himself, Jack smiled. "As I recall, you won your share in those days."

Pete gestured to the open door across the reception area. "Come on back. Let's talk about today," he said patting Jack's shoulder.

Jack winced and quickened his pace.

Pete closed the door and motioned Jack to a seat on the couch in the corner. "I've been out for two weeks," Jack began, "and came back to find two listing presentations being prepared for you by brokers in my office. I understand one of them's got an appointment to present to you this afternoon, but the other one's the designated team."

Worry lines formed on Pete's forehead. "Jesus, I'm sorry. I was afraid this might happen. Thompson told me that you had appointed Paul and Brent Jensen. I just couldn't see Paul working on a bunch of little buildings and I couldn't imagine Brent carrying the project without him. So after I was asked to manage the property, I had a little conversation with Liz Peterson. I'm really comfortable with her. When I talked to Liz about it, I told her that the Jensens had been designated and that I wanted to talk to you about assigning her to the project. Liz said you were out of town for two weeks and not to worry about it, she'd take care of it. I presumed it was all done. Didn't she talk to Miles?"

Jack nodded slowly. "Yeah, Pete, Liz spoke with Miles while I was gone. But you didn't speak to Paul Jensen. He tells me he's got several unreturned calls into you."

There was silence between the two men for a few seconds. "What would you like to do?" Pete asked.

"I'd like you and Dick and I to have a conversation, so we're all on the same page."

A frown flashed across Pete's face.

Jack smiled pleasantly. "That okay with you?"

"Of course."

Jack pointed across the room to the phone on Pete's desk. "Think we could call him now?"

Pete stood, walked across the room, picked up the phone and dialed Thompson's number. After a brief conversation with the secretary, he hung up. "Thompson's out and she can't get hold of him. He's due back at one-thirty. He'll be there very briefly, and then he'll be on his way out here for Liz's presentation at three."

Jack rose. "Okay, we'll postpone the presentation."

Lines again became visible across Pete's forehead. "If that's what you want, Jack. It's your show."

"Thompson charged me with a decision and I gave him the Jensen's. I need to be certain we're all in agreement before there's any change."

"Of course," Pete responded. "You'll tell Liz?"

"I'll tell her." Jack moved toward the door. "And I'll put in a call to Dick."

Pete moved toward the door to see Jack off.

At the door Jack stopped. "As soon as we've talked this through, we'll reschedule."

Pete didn't comment.

*   *   *

The new Seville sped away from the parking lot of the Clarion Hotel and within a block accelerated onto the freeway toward downtown Los Angeles. Duran lounged in the passenger seat, his eyes covered by a pair of ski glasses with orange day-glo lenses. The glasses and his languid tension gave him the presence of a preying mantis. A preying mantis with a gold Rolex.

"What did you make of that, Segundo?" he inquired of the driver.

"Some of them loved having you back. One or two are tense," came the response.

"One or two of them should be." He paused. "What do you make of the management team?"

"Preston makes a great master of ceremonies. He's got the look, but he's an empty suit if you ask me."

"Who else could I be asking, asshole?" Duran shot back. The corners of his mouth turned up as he said it. His eyes glowed orange. "What about what's his name—Kendrick?"

"Don't have a clue. Didn't speak a word to the man. He shot out of there like a scalded dog. Wonder what the hell he was in such a rush about?"

"I bet I know. He's covering his ass."

The driver looked over his right shoulder quizzically.

"The road, Segundo. Watch the road," Duran commanded.

The driver turned forward. On the radio, a talk show host debated with a caller. Duran put his head back against the headrest, deep in thought. "Preston's got to go."

"Can't handle the office?" Duran's lieutenant asked.

"No he can't, but that's not the problem," Duran answered. "The problem is a whole lot more urgent than that. He's my boss's boy. Can't have the guy running my biggest office in the position to go over my head at Sunday afternoon cookouts, now can I?"

"May be a problem, but there's not much you can do about it. The pres is gonna protect his boy, isn't he?"

"Same as I'd protect you, Segundo. Same as I'd protect you." Duran pointed at the radio. "Shut that communist mother-fucker up. LA's got to be the last city in America to let a bed-wetting, communist prick like that host a morning talk show."

The driver snapped the power button and the car was silent except for the sound of the air conditioner.

"He may be our illustrious president's pal, but he's vulnerable. Used up all his old boy chits in the spanking," Duran explained.

"Spanking? What the fuck are you talking about?"

"Segundo, you must be the only guy in the company that hasn't heard the story. At an office birthday party, one of the secretaries dabbed icing from a cake on his nose, and the old fart lost it. He grabbed her, sat down, turned her over his knee and spanked her," Duran explained. "Christ, I heard about it. I was in Phoenix at the time trying to raise money to build some more of these vacant turkeys surrounding us." He waved out the window toward a group of low flat warehouse structures.

"No shit? He spanked her?" The driver said and laughed. "Old boy must have sprung a diamond-cutter like he hadn't had in years."

Both men laughed.

"How'd he get away with it?" the driver asked.

"Ah, the pres bailed him out," explained Duran. "But like I said, I think Preston used up all his ol' buddy chits in the process. I can get rid of him if I set it up right."

"How about all this Paul and Liz shit we keep hearing?" suggested the driver. "There's got to be a way to use that."

"Preston's a cagey old bird. He's doing his best not to get caught between those two or make a decision that will piss one of them off," Duran said. "In fact, it's obvious he's forcing all the hard calls on Kendrick."

"I got it!"

Duran turned and stared through preying mantis eyes. "Got what?"

"If Kendrick's making the tough calls, and he's Preston's boy, take 'em both down."

"Keep talking," commanded Duran.

"Kendrick's gonna fuck up at least once in this mess. When he does, bring him down. But rather than letting Preston distance himself from Kendrick, tie them together. Simple."

Duran's lips turned up again. "I like the way you think, Segundo."

CHAPTER 15

"We've Cut Our Nuts Off"

WHEN JACK arrived at his office, he called Dick Thompson's secretary and said it was very important that Thompson contact him as soon as possible. He then tried Thompson's car phone.

"The party you are trying to reach is outside the service area or away from the vehicle," came the response from the cellular phone company.

Jack tried Dick's home number. What's Mrs. Thompson's name? Think. A woman's voice answered, "Hello."

"June?" he asked, hesitantly.

"Yes?" came the equally hesitant reply.

"June, this is Jack Kendrick. Remember me?"

"Sure, Jack, I remember, and Dick's mentioned you a few times lately."

"June, I'm sorry to trouble you at home, but I need to get hold of him. Could you ask him to call me?"

"Sure, Jack. I'll ask him to call."

There was nothing more to do but wait.

* * *

Jack could see Liz's clenched jaw as she marched into his office. "You canceled our meeting!"

He tried to keep his expression bland. "Sit down."

She stood as though deciding if she had an option. After a

moment's hesitation she sat down and scissored one black-nyloned leg over the other.

"Yes, I canceled your meeting," Jack said.

Silence fell as they locked eyeballs.

"Why?" she asked angrily.

"Because I'm not sure you're making the presentation." Jack kept his voice soft and flat.

"What's that supposed to mean?" Liz asked.

Jack leaned forward and crossed his forearms on the desk. "Liz, I appointed a broker to do this presentation. It wasn't you. I came back and found you and the Jensens getting ready to pitch. It's not going to happen."

Liz threw her hands up. "National Commerce Bank hired Pete Mastrionni as their manager and now the decision's his. It's a new deal."

Jack stared at her. "I'm not so sure. NCB hired a property manager. Dick Thompson is still making the decision. What's changed is that you've positioned yourself into the deal."

"Horseshit," Liz exploded. "I didn't position myself into this deal. Pete invited me in. He said if Jensen were in, we'd lose. And Pete said he was making the decision."

Jack eased back from his desk just a bit. "Liz, neither Pete Mastrionni nor Dick Thompson tells me that Pete is making this decision. Nothing is going to happen here until I have just one representative on this. The one I pick."

"You wanna pick, you pick," she spat. "But you don't pick me, we'll lose." She crossed her arms over her chest and looked at him with an expression of white heat. She rose to leave as abruptly as she had come in. "It doesn't matter anyhow. All we've managed to do is look weak and confused. We've cut our nuts off." She left. The sound of her heels drummed a diminishing tattoo on the tile as she stormed away.

Thompson called shortly after. "I understand this afternoon's presentation has been canceled." He sounded surprised. "It appears the defecation's hit the rotary oscillator at your place. What's going on?"

Jack tried to sound calm. "I'd like to talk to you about it, but I'd much rather do it face to face. Can I come down to your office this afternoon?"

"I'm on the way back from San Diego. I was going to drive straight to Pete's office for our three o'clock. No reason for that now. I'm gonna go home. I'll be there around three. Why don't you come by? I'll introduce you to my first born if he's not napping. You remember where I live?"

"I remember."

Before leaving Jack stopped in Miles' office.

Miles put his hands behind his bald head and rocked his chair back as if studying the ceiling. "Paul's been on the losing end of several deals lately. More than one to his ex-protégé. Stick with him if you can."

Jack thought he was past being amazed at Miles' ability to blow with the wind. "What the hell are you talking about?"

Miles abruptly rocked forward and brought his arms down.

Jack bored in. "When Liz came in to tell you she was going to make the presentation, did you tell her not to, that Paul was in charge?"

Miles looked blankly at Jack. "No. Why?"

"Did you tell Paul that he was no longer representing ACRE on the deal?"

"No," Miles answered, unruffled.

Jack struggled to keep his voice in control. "Well, were you going to allow two presentations? How did you expect to handle it?"

"I knew you'd deal with it when you got back," Miles said. "That's your job, Jack."

*　　*　　*

The thing Jack remembered most about Thompson's house was the hole in his garage door. It was patched now, but Jack could still

see the outline. Thompson bought the house from a weekend sail-
or who had trailered a sailboat too long to fit into the garage. Too
long, by about one foot. Rather than leave the boat outside or
the garage door up, he'd cut a hole in the door, and let the bowsprit stick out. When Thompson moved in he'd patched the hole.
The patch still showed and brought a smile as Jack walked up the
drive.

June answered the door, and directed Jack through the small
foyer to Thompson's study. Jack was surprised to see him in a pair
of pink baggy shorts with large, white hibiscus flowers imprinted
on them. A white T-shirt with a small rip near the collar covered
his large torso. Thompson was barefoot and his receding blonde
hair disheveled. He was on the phone and engaged in energetic
conversation with someone at his office. Jack was sure whoever
was on the other end envisioned Thompson in a gray suit and not
pink hibiscus-print shorts.

As soon as the conversation ended, Thompson jumped up, extended his large hand and let a warm smile sweep across his broad
face. After hellos, Thompson led him to the new baby's room
where they spoke with whispered delight around the crib. It was
the skinniest baby Jack had ever seen, and he wondered if he could
possibly grow up to be as burly as his daddy.

Finally, they tiptoed out of the nursery. Thompson grabbed
two Dos Equis from the refrigerator and the men went back to the
study.

"Why'd you cancel the presentation?" Thompson asked as
they settled into a pair of mismatched overstuffed chairs.

"Who'd you expect to be there?" Jack answered with a question.

Thompson took a long swallow from his beer. "Pete and I on
our side. You and your broker on yours."

"What broker did you think I was bringing?"

"Until yesterday when you called," Dick answered, "I thought
it was the Jensens. Those were the guys you picked. Paul called me

to set up the presentation, and I told him Pete was handling the logistics and to call him. Before Pete left for San Francisco, he called and said the ACRE presentation had been scheduled for today."

"Did he say with who?"

"No," Thompson continued. "I presumed the Jensens. Until your call yesterday. What the fuck is this all about?"

Jack picked up his beer. "Pete never called Paul Jensen back." He pulled on the bottle and set it back down. "He did, however, set up a presentation with Liz Peterson. That's who was scheduled today at three."

Thompson's face froze. Jack felt amused by such a serious expression on the face of a man wearing pink hibiscus shorts.

"You've got a problem," he finally said.

Jack nodded and then shrugged.

"You're gonna end up with egg on your face if Liz gets the assignment after you designated the Jensens. My guy Mastrionni seems to have put you in a bit of a mess. Have you and he talked about it?"

"First thing this morning," Jack answered. "I put off the presentation because I wanted us all in agreement before we went forward."

"Your pick is the Jensens, and Pete's is Liz."

"What's yours?"

Thompson ran his fingers through thinning blond hair, and scratched his scalp. "Truth is, Jack, I know Liz by reputation only. Never met her." He paused a moment. "But I hear she's unstoppable."

"Do you want her on the project?" Jack studied his face.

"Would she do a better job than the Jensens?"

"I doubt it."

"You sure?"

A large silver framed picture of Dick and June Thompson dressed in their wedding regalia caught his eye. Jack studied it for a moment. "You remember when you proposed?" Jack gestured to the picture on the desk beside Dick.

Thompson turned momentarily to look at the picture to which Jack pointed. "Yeah, I remember." He smiled and turned back to Jack. "Why?"

"Were you nervous?"

"Yeah. Sure."

"Any reservations?" Jack asked.

"No. She was the one." A smile played across Thompson's lips as though he were lost in happy memory.

"None. No reservations at all?"

"I can't imagine a guy not having some doubts, but I was right. It turned out fine." Thompson's concentration snapped back. "I see where you're going with this."

There was a momentary silence in the room as both men sipped at their beers.

"So, who's it gonna be?" Thompson broke the silence.

Jack swallowed the last of his beer, and set the empty on the table beside his chair. "Let's reschedule for Friday. Same time. Same place. I'll let you know before then."

The man in the pink hibiscus shorts nodded agreement.

*   *   *

Jack played the voice mail back again.

"This is Jim Duran. We didn't get a chance to meet at breakfast. I'd like to talk to you. Stop by my office tomorrow morning around seven o'clock. See you then."

"*Beeepp*. You have no further messages in your mail box."

Now there's one hell of a message.

CHAPTER 16

Hegelian Dialectic

BETWEEN daybreak and sunrise, the steel and glass canyons of downtown Los Angeles filled with a flat shadowless light that reminded Jack of dawn in the steep river canyons on the western slope of the Sierra Nevada. He drove into the open parking lot in the corporate headquarters building, but the guard made him sign in before he'd let him ride the elevator up. When he got off at the top, Jack's eyebrows rose in surprise. Two massive wooden doors blocked the hallway to the executive offices. The few times Jack had visited here, he hadn't noticed them. Well, he thought, I've never been here this early.

Jack tested the doors and found them locked. He rapped sharply, hoping someone inside would let him in. He'd like a cup of coffee before he met Duran. No one answered, so he spent the next fifteen minutes standing in the gloomy hallway in front of the bank of elevators. At exactly 7:00 a.m., the same guard who'd made him sign in appeared from the fire exit and opened the doors guarding the executive suites.

It irritated Jack to find the lights on and occupants in several of the offices. They either had not heard, or ignored, his knock. He walked back toward the Division Manager's office.

Duran sat with his jacket off, his sleeves rolled up, a half-filled cup of coffee perched atop the cluttered stack of papers that covered his desktop, and a telephone frozen to his ear. Three windows along each of two walls gave the office a spacious, airy feeling as well as an expansive view of the heliport on the adjacent rooftop and the streets below, now starting to clog with morning traffic. A couch and over-stuffed chair covered in the same fabric and a lacquered wood coffee table filled the corner space. His desk formed a protective fortress between Duran and the rest of the room.

Duran didn't rise or interrupt his monologue, but he did motion Jack to the vacant seat across the desk from him. He maintained unblinking eye contact with Jack as he spoke into the receiver. Jack tried to hide his unease at this adolescent game of stare down. "Listen, partner, this shit with eighty dollar lunches for staff will stop as of now," Duran growled. "We agreed your expenses would come down. That means all of them. You understand? 'Cause if you don't, I'll take over your whole damn expense budget, and you'll like that a lot less than you like this. If that isn't crystal clear you call me soon as you get in. Bye."

Jack couldn't suppress a small smile thinking Duran had chewed out the miscreant's voice mail.

Duran didn't return the smile. "What's all this shit I hear about National Commerce Bank?" he snapped as he dropped the receiver into its cradle.

He listened attentively as Jack told the tale.

When Jack got to the part relating to the selection of the marketing team, Duran pounced. "Well, what the hell are you going to do about it?"

Jack tried to stay calm and not get sucked in by Duran's outburst. "I'm going to stick with the Jensens."

"What the fuck would you do that for?" Duran demanded.

Jack couldn't tell if Duran disagreed or if he was testing. He maintained contact with the small brown eyes that peered at him and wished he had that cup of coffee. "Because I assigned them to the job."

"So?"

Jack decided he might enjoy this. "So, company policy, not to mention the National Association Code of Ethics, says one salesperson will not attempt to insert himself into another salesperson's transaction."

"They don't say a manager can't change his pick. You put 'em on; you can take 'em off."

Jack slowed. He uncrossed his ankles and straightened in his chair. "If I do, everyone will know it was because I was forced to."

"By who?"

Jack let his skepticism show a bit. "Authority is a precious commodity for any sales manager. For one who doesn't pay his people a dime, and takes half of what they bring in, it's critical."

"What the fuck are you talking about?"

Duran understood, and Jack knew it. "I'm talking about who's in charge. Is it me, or is it the big hitters?"

Duran studied him for a moment. "Partner, I've just come back, but let me tell you how I see things. Your revenues are going down like the Titanic. Your two stars want to see each other lose more than they want to win, and there's no one at the helm. Fuckin' Preston is a figurehead and not much more. Clear enough so far?"

Jack said nothing.

"Hear this next part real clear," Duran said. "I hold you responsible for what happens out there. And your number one mission is to stop revenues from slipping. You lose any more big ones, and your ass will be gone within the week. Got it, partner?"

Jack knew there wasn't any help or understanding coming from Duran. "You could not have made yourself clearer," he answered.

Duran took a sip of coffee, set the cup down and picked up his stack of messages. The meeting had ended, and Jack rose to go.

Duran looked back up. His expression reflected benign indifference. "A word of advice."

Jack straightened to his full height and tried to match Duran's expression.

"Jensen is the past; Liz is the future."

* * *

Jack navigated the four-level interchange and caught the San Bernardino Freeway as though on automatic pilot. *I don't think I've been upbraided that completely since bootcamp.* He tried hard to stay still and let the adrenaline wash through him.

Asshole. Liz runs roughshod through the office and people's lives.

Oh, for Christ sake, Jack, you don't know that. She had a pretty reasonable story about Montgomery, and she is the broker Pete Mastrionni wants. And when things took a major twist, while you were on vacation, she did see Miles about it. You're just on your high horse 'cause she didn't respect your authority.

But Paul and Brent Jensen sure haven't done much to win over NCB since Patch moved up. And, Jack, old buddy, what Duran gave you back there was as close to a direct order as you're ever going to get. And you do need this job. Lizzy wins.

Jack realized he had to piss. He'd be to his office in another thirty minutes if no one in front of him had a wreck.

He'd decided and now he'd have to inform the Jensens. What a pain in the ass that would be. Jack believed in having the tough conversation first, so he'd tell each of them before he told Liz. *God, he needed to piss.*

By the time Jack pulled into the parking lot he was holding his knees together and could think of nothing but the pressure in his bladder. He screeched to a halt in the handicapped stall right in front of the main entrance. *I'll be back out in three minutes to move it. No chance of the $247 ticket guy getting here before I get back.*

He walked to the building at a pace far more rapid than dignity would have dictated, but managed to cross the lobby to the men's room before anyone saw him. He threw the door open and unzipped his fly as he rushed toward the line of three urinals against the far wall. The one in the middle was occupied. Jack recognized the broad back, thick waist and neck and the sandy, waved hair combed to try to cover the bare spot on the top. Paul Jensen stood with an elbow draped over each of the dividing partitions. The no hands technique. Why do guys do that? Is it a statement? "My flaccid dick is so long it hangs out my fly and below my crotch. I have no fear of peeing on my pants, so I don't have to hold it."

"Move an elbow big guy, and make way for a newcomer."

The unblinking green eyes turned to stare at him even as the intruding elbow disappeared.

"You may turn out to be a decent sales manager after all."

Jack worked at his fly for a moment and then looked up and returned the stare. "Thanks for the compliment, but mind telling me what's led to this sudden appreciation?" Jack tried to relax so the flow could start and the pressure subside.

"I heard that back-stabbing bitch tried to position herself into the Cunningham presentation, and you found out and flat canceled the whole thing. I like guys who do the right thing."

Relax. Relax. "It's the Inland Industrial Park now Paul… Ahh." Jack's spine straightened and his head relaxed backward. "And don't thank me yet."

"What's that mean?"

"NCB changed the name of the project, Paul. They no longer refer to it as the Cunningham Project. It's the Inland Industrial Park." Jack felt his facial muscles relax. The flow made a steady satisfying ring against the porcelain.

"I understood that part," Paul growled. "What's 'don't thank me yet' supposed to mean?" Paul looked at the tile inches in front of his face. Both hands dropped from the partitions and his shoulders folded slightly forward.

"It means I stopped the presentation until I could figure out what the hell was going on. I have and it's back on."

Jack heard the sound of Paul's zipper, and the big man next to him stepped back behind his peripheral vision. His footfalls echoed off the tile floor. "Her or me?"

Jack stared at the tile. "Her, Paul."

"You useless son of a bitch," came the howl from behind him.

Jack zipped up his trousers, and turned to see Paul twist on the water faucet full bore. Water splashed out of the basin and poured over the front of Paul's pants.

"God damn it!" Paul snapped off the faucet and grabbed a handful of paper towels, which he wiped down over his soaked pants.

Jack cautiously approached the other basin. "Look, Paul, I'm sorry, but the client wants Liz," he said addressing the bald spot on the top of Paul's head.

Paul wiped down the counter before he straightened, a wad of wet towels still in his hand. A very tense silence fell as the two men stared. "So you're going to cave in," Paul said, his voice in control. "You're going to shit-can the Jensens and placate Liz."

Jack fought the temptation to justify himself to those piercing green eyes. "Paul, I'm not placating Liz. I'm trying to get the business for the American Corporate Real Estate Company."

The cords in Paul's thick neck stood out. His face flushed. "I'm out and that placates Liz! And it's wrong." He threw the wad of towels past Jack's head. They flattened into the wall with a splat.

Jack turned to watch the soggy mass slide down the wall to the floor. He turned back to Paul's angry face.

"I don't mind so much for me," Paul said, his voice echoing off the tiles, "but there's no God-damn reason my son should be penalized because I've got enemies. Brent's a hard workin' young man. This project's perfect for him. He should be on it!"

Jack felt sympathy for a parent who believed his son was paying for his mistakes. Brent might be good on this. Paul had a point. He might be right about the rest too. Jack turned to wash his hands. Paul had fallen silent, but Jack could feel his eyes burning into the side of his face. "I can't help you and Brent if you won't help yourselves."

"And just exactly what's that supposed to mean?"

"When your old clients choose to do business with Liz instead of you, what the hell do you expect me to do about it?"

"T.T. Armenquest wouldn't pick her over me in a hundred years."

"Paul, it's not T.T. It's Mastrionni; he's got the say on this one."

"That sleazy little bastard would follow a skirt anywhere!"

"Ah, come on, Paul. Mastrionni isn't the only one who's picked her lately." Jack was exasperated.

"Yeah, I forgot. Cornhole picked her too," he spat. "I never was his type."

"Who?"

"Oscar Cornblatt. 'Cornhole' to everyone in the business."

Jack said nothing.

"Cornhole, Jack." Paul spoke as though explaining to a child. Then he licked the end of his little finger and ran it over an arched eyebrow. "He's a light-in-the-loafer, limp-wristed, friend of Dorothy's, and everyone knows it." His voice started to rise. "If Liz wants to play fag-hag to him, let her, but don't imply she's doing a better job than I am because of it." Paul took a step toward Jack and thrust his face forward until their noses were inches apart. "You're rewarding the bitch for violating your directive and going around the team you picked. It's not right, God-damn it!" Paul shouted.

The door opened and one of the young associates appeared. He looked from Paul to Jack. "'Scuse me. I'll come back later." He backed out hastily.

Jack remained motionless for a moment, wiped the edge of the counter top with a paper towel and propped his hip against it. "Paul, do you know who Hegel is?"

Paul blinked in confusion. "Hegel? The philosopher?"

"Yeah." Jack gave just a hint of a smile. "Eighteenth-century German philosopher."

Paul continued to look combative. "What about him?"

"He made an interesting observation. His predecessors saw things as either true or false. Hegel didn't. He saw truth as dynamic—constantly developing, changing."

"Sounds as spineless as you."

Jack ignored the insult and continued. "He said truth stood only until its opposite, its antithesis, developed. Hegel said right and wrong weren't absolute. Instead, the two combine into a new reality, a synthesis." Jack paused.

Paul stood rigid. His arms folded across his chest. "What the fuck has that got to do with this?"

"Everything, Paul, 'cause what we've got here is a synthesis. It may be wrong for you, but it's not wrong for the rest of the world. It's what the client wants; it's what's gonna happen."

Paul's lips curled and his eyebrows rose as he spoke. "Jack, I'm just a country boy. In Elko they didn't teach much Hegel. But they did teach a lot of life, and I've lived a lot of it. And there are things that are right and there are things that are wrong, and this is wrong."

Paul's blazing green eyes stared hard for what seemed like forever directly into Jack's eyes. He looked old, haggard and defeated, but still defiant. Jack resisted the urge to turn away—to give up to the challenge. He managed to return the stare.

"You think you're gonna take a million dollars out of my pocket, and turn it into a virtue, 'cause you ain't got the balls to stand up to that bitch," Paul finally said. "Unlike you, I'm glad I won't have to look myself in the mirror every morning with that lie." He walked very slowly and held himself very erect as he left the room.

* * *

Jack dreaded the conversation with Liz. Despite his comments to Paul, he didn't relish admitting to Liz that he'd acquiesced. So he felt relief when Irene said Liz would be out all day. Jack thought about calling her in the car, but he really wanted to talk with Brent first, so he put it off.

Brent didn't come in. Late in the afternoon, Jack tried his car phone. "We need to talk," Jack said when Brent answered.

"About what?" came the sullen reply.

"The Inland Industrial Park." Jack waited for a response. None came. "Brent, you there?"

"I'm here; I'm just not sure what's to talk about."

Jack let the comment hang in the air.

"If you insist," Brent acquiesced.

"I do."

"When?"

"How about this evening?"

"Gonna work out," came Brent's curt reply.

"Great. Join me for a run in Palos Verdes," Jack invited.

"Okay. Parking lot at Malaga Cove about six-thirty."

"If you can't keep up, I'll blame it on your youth and lack of experience," Jack said.

"I'll keep up, Dude."

CHAPTER 17

Alpha Male

MALAGA COVE PLAZA is not only the prettiest strip center in Los Angeles; it's arguably the only pretty strip center in Los Angeles. It
has the traditional L-shape of strip centers, but the resemblance
ends there. The Plaza is a two-story brick affair with the upper
story extending out over the lower. The cantilevered second story
is supported by an arched colonnade that creates a shaded walk for
the shops below. The second story is populated with the offices of
CPAs, financial advisors and divorce attorneys. The shops on the
ground floor include art galleries, antique stores, residential real
estate offices and two banks. It serves the needs of the local community.

A fifteen-foot-high fountain stands in the middle of the parking lot. Atop its white marble, baroque splendor, the naked figure
of Poseidon, posed trident in hand, commands dominion over the
European luxury sedans parked below. Poseidon is raised on a
three-tiered pedestal covered with gargoyles and putti. The pedestal is supported by four mermaids, each riding a dolphin. Their
nipples spray water into the pool.

The pool draws joggers, who find it perfect for stretching before and after running along the equestrian trails that crisscross the
hill that rise a thousand feet above the Plaza.

When Jack arrived, Brent was already in his running gear and stretching. Jack parked beside Brent's four-wheel-drive Toyota truck, said hello and did a quick change in the back seat. He was careful not to offend any passing dowagers by getting caught between boxers and running shorts.

The two men jogged along the Palos Verdes Drive until they turned onto an equestrian trail that ran along the top of the bluff. On their right were the backyard fences of some of the most expensive homes in the world. On their left the bluff dropped a hundred feet to the rooftops of Torrance. The dirt trail did a slow ascent for two miles along the bluff.

"Brent," Jack asked when their pace settled into the rhythm of long distance running, "have you talked to your dad today?"

Brent turned to look over his shoulder at the older man half a pace behind "I know you've dumped us, if that's what you mean."

Jack tried to catch Brent's eye, but the younger man turned his face to the path. He spoke to the rear of Brent's head. "You've got the 'what' of it. I thought we might talk about the 'why'."

Brent didn't turn around. "Okay, why?"

"You know that NCB hired Armenquest to manage the property. Thompson and Mastrionni are making this decision together. Pete thinks your dad is a big deal guy and won't work all these little buildings. He thinks Liz will. So he wants Liz. Thompson goes along."

The trail rose sharply for twenty yards and Jack stopped talking while he labored up the slope.

"How do you s'pose Pete got so opinionated?" Brent asked.

Jack didn't want to answer. He wanted to concentrate on his breathing. To relax and be loose. "If you're asking whether I think Liz positioned herself into the deal? Yeah, probably." Jack wanted Brent to talk, but he said nothing. Jack was uncomfortable. This hurt. "But if she did, she did an awfully fine job of it. The client wants her."

"And that's it?" Brent snorted. "That's what the client wants so we're out? You," Brent turned to glare at him. "You designated us and Liz positioned herself against your directive? But she did such a good job," Brent's voice rolled sarcasm, "that the company policy, which says she must honor our position, doesn't matter. Fuckin' terrific!"

When they had reached the top of the two-mile grade they broke off the equestrian trail and ran through a neighborhood of meandering streets and cul-de-sacs, lined with large stuccoed homes with red Tuscan-tiled roofs. They ran without speaking. Finally, they found themselves at the top of a narrow ravine. White limestone formed walls that rose above them as they descended into the arroyo. Tall stalks of anise rose in full bloom and threatened to snap of their own weight. The setting sun reflected off the white walls creating a magical quality. A licorice-like aroma hung densely in the air around them. The shrill "Kee Aww" of a feral peacock in the canyon below pierced the stillness.

"Ever take biology?" Brent asked.

Jack felt more comfortable speaking, as they ran downhill. "Yeah, a fair amount. That was before I flunked organic chemistry and discovered I was going to have to find some path through life besides veterinary medicine."

The younger man smiled. "Know the term 'alpha male'?"

Jack thought for a second. "Wolves?" he asked.

"That's right," Brent said. "Wolves. Packs are pretty structured. There's one male—big dude—who runs things. Leads the hunts and like that. He gets the best meat and pick of the females."

They had finally reached the bottom of the ravine, which opened up into a small box canyon. There was a little stable and a few corrals in the middle. The trail ran through the corrals and then zigzagged up the canyon wall.

Brent continued, "Know what happens when he starts to get old?"

"You tell me."

"Young studs come after 'em. Eventually, one of 'em whips his ass. Know what happens then?"

Jack labored hard up the steep switchbacks. "What?" was all he grunted out.

"Winner is the new alpha male and gets all the good shit that comes with the job." The pace seemed easy for Brent. "Old guy keeps getting whipped. All of 'em want at least one bite out of his ass. Old guy usually doesn't stay around long. Kinda wanders off to die alone."

They continued running for a few minutes in silence. "All that meaning what?" Jack asked.

Brent turned his head for a moment to look quizzically at Jack. "Pretty obvious, isn't it? I think that's what they're doing to my dad. He's not as aggressive as he once was. And they're chewing him up—starting with her." After a few moments of silence Brent added, "It's not right."

Jack's attention came off the pain in his diaphragm, and he stared at the curly-blond head in front of him, surprised it held any thought that deep.

A small municipal park lined with eucalyptus trees greeted them at the top of the canyon wall. Bougainvillea and wisteria climbed tall fences around the tennis courts. The two runners crossed the park, turned west and headed back toward Malaga Cove Plaza. Now they gave back all the altitude they'd gained in the last forty minutes. A mile-and-a-half of steady downhill lay before them; a runner's dream. Their pace increased as they started down.

"You think that analogy really applies?" Jack looked at Brent's profile momentarily. "You think we're all a bunch of wolves? That success is just getting the most—the most deals, the most women? And the guy on top gets 'em?"

Brent gave him a baleful look but said nothing. They soon finished their long downhill and ran across the parking lot up to the statue. They walked around to cool down and then stretched at the fountain.

Brent looked up. "One thing I want to be clear about."

Jack stretched out over his leg and studied him.

"The reason you dumped us was because Liz had done such a good job of positioning herself that the client insisted. Right?"

Jack felt the tension as he stretched his leg across the fountain ledge. "That's about right."

"And you agree that proper procedure would have been for her to stay the hell out after you designated us?"

Jack's discomfort increased. He wanted to be done with this. "Yeah. That's right, too."

"So you rewarded Liz for doing wrong?"

Jack removed his leg from the fountain and spoke very gently. "Brent, if I hadn't done that, I don't think we'd have a chance to get that account."

Brent's stare was almost penetrating. "So you made a decision for the money rather than for what was right."

*   *   *

Jack saw the two young men shooting baskets in the driveway so he pulled up at the curb and parked behind the aging Honda Civic with a patch of orange Bondo on the rear fender.

"Hi, Dad. Been for a run?" the lanky blond youth called out as Jack walked up the drive, briefcase in one hand and his clothes hanging over his other arm.

"Observant as ever," Jack responded.

"Dad, you remember Jamie Escobar?" Ian asked, reintroducing father and friend.

"Hi, Jamie." Jack set down his briefcase and extended a hand to Ian's equally lanky friend. "Nice to see you again. You staying for dinner?"

"Hi, Mr. K," Jamie responded. "Thanks, but no thanks. Ian and I have dates this evening. We're doubling."

"Now that Ian has his license," Jack pointed with a smile toward the Honda, "and wheels, and you still have that Exhibition of Speed hanging over you, I suspect this doubling will continue for a while." And then he said to Ian, "A date in the middle of the week, must mean I can expect a report card with nothing but A's this semester." Jack reached toward the basketball in Ian's hand.

Ian handed it to him. "All except for Stratton's government class."

Jack raised the ball over his head with one hand; his suit and tie still awkwardly draped over his other arm. He launched the ball and watched it arc toward the basket. It sailed short, missing the entire basket and bouncing off the garage door.

"Airball!" both boys taunted in unison.

Jack shrugged his shoulders and picked up his briefcase. "Do you want to talk about Stratton's class now?"

"Later."

Jack walked toward the front door. "Say good-bye before you go," he called without looking back.

"Will do, Dad."

Jack wandered through the tiled entry and let his nose and habit lead him to the kitchen. "Hi, honey. How was your day?" he asked.

"Fine, sweetie," she said looking up from a simmering pot. "How was yours?"

"A two hundred and forty-seven dollar parking ticket aside, it was interesting."

"A what?" she sounded incredulous.

"Long story. I'll tell you later."

"For two hundred and forty-seven dollars, it better be a good story." Her hazel eyes twinkled merriment. "Did Ian tell you his SATs came back?"

Jack walked around the chopping block in the middle of the room and headed toward her. "No, all he commented on was my jump shot. How'd he do?" Jack asked as he reached for her.

"No hugs for you. Not until you shower or at least put on a dry shirt." Lorna held her hand between them with her index fingers crossed. "He didn't say. I think he wants to tell you himself."

"Well, I guess not with Jamie here, he doesn't. I wonder if that's good or bad."

"Don't know," Lorna responded and gave him a quick peck on the lips. "You take a quick shower. I'll have dinner ready by the time you're out. Just the two of us tonight."

"Two's good. I want your opinion on something. Back in ten minutes," he said as he went off to the shower.

"Alfresco tonight," she called after him.

When Jack walked onto the patio, the first thing he noticed was the shot glass of dark amber liquid beside his plate. He sipped, savored the very strong peat flavor of the Laphroig, exhaled and sat down smiling.

"You said you wanted my opinion on something. Thought you might want a scotch as well."

"How'd you know that?" he asked.

"A woman knows these things. Now tell me."

"Liz is screwing me."

"Figuratively, I trust."

Jack grinned. "Not my type."

"What's she do?"

Jack sipped from the shot glass and rolled the liquor around on his tongue. When he swallowed, it warmed him from his center to his ribs. "Duran told me that if I didn't assign her, and we lost the NCB deal, he'd fire me."

"Ouch! Guess we're going to need that severance pay from So Cal Commercial after all."

He studied her as she said it. If Lorna was concerned, it didn't show in her expression, tone or posture. Jack picked up his fork and rearranged the pasta on his plate. Without looking up, he answered her. "No, honey, I caved." His voice was barely above a whisper. "I told the Jensens they were out."

Lorna rose and walked around behind him. She put one hand on his cheek and gently pulled Jack's head back until it nestled between her breasts. She stroked his hair. "So what's the question you want my opinion on?"

"Am I doing the right thing?"

"Of course you are," she answered immediately.

He turned to look up at her smile.

"That one's easy. I thought you were going to ask me a tough one."

"Honey, this is tough. Young Jensen showed some intellect this afternoon. Accused me of selling out my standards to chase a deal."

She stroked his head again. "This is so tough on my warrior." Lorna stroked him one last time and then left. She came back a few minutes later with two mugs of coffee giving off wispy fumes and pungent odors into the evening air. She swept his almost untouched dinner plate to the middle of the table, put down the mugs, pulled out the chair beside him. Then she sat down, and picked up the conversation as though she'd never left. "You really don't like being forced, do you?"

"Huh?"

"Jack, the facts that Jim Duran is threatening to fire you, and that Liz Peterson went around you to get her way, do not, by themselves, mean that doing what they want is wrong. Particularly," she continued, "when Paul Jensen hasn't done enough to impress the client and the client is asking for Liz."

Jack held the mug in both hands and blew across the top, as much to watch the steam swirl where the heat from the coffee met the moist sea air, as to cool it. "For the sake of discussion I'll give you all that. But how about the question of wickedness?"

"Wickedness?"

"Paul tells me Oscar Cornblatt is homosexual."

Lorna arched an eyebrow. "So?"

"I don't care what Cornblatt's sex life is like. None of my business." He sipped at the still steaming mug. "I don't care what he and Montgomery did that night as long as Montgomery was happy to do it. But suppose, just suppose she set Montgomery up—forced him to have sex with Cornblatt—just to make a deal, some more money."

"Honey, if she did, you're right. She is evil and you fight her. But you don't know that. Her side of the story is pretty reasonable."

"Then why'd she leave him there?" Jack asked.

"She told you. They were having a good time, the two men. She's a mom. She needed to get home."

"Well, there's some damn reason that boy killed himself!" Jack banged his fist on the table.

Lorna sat looking at him until the echo of the table service rattling evaporated into the moist sea air. "There's one part of the story that just doesn't fit in with that version."

Jack sipped coffee and studied his calm and beautiful wife.

"If Liz Peterson had all this control over the guy, why'd she let him buy a building where she had to split a commission?"

Jack couldn't bring the question into focus. "What?"

"Didn't you say she made about seventy-five thousand dollars?" Lorna asked.

Jack nodded.

"And the building was listed with some other broker who also made seventy-five thousand dollars. And didn't you tell me that there are buildings out there where the seller has no broker and all of the commission is paid to the buyer's broker?"

"All true," Jack agreed.

"So if she's so doggone interested in what's good for her, at everyone else's expense, and she used that poor kid to get control over old Cornhole—"

"Lorna," Jack feigned surprise.

"Well he is, right?"

Jack nodded.

"Why didn't she sell him a building where she could make one hundred and fifty thousand dollars instead of only seventy-five?"

"That's a real good question," Jack said. "If she used Montgomery to develop total control of Cornblatt, she'd have steered him to a building where she could get the full pop."

"Exactly. Honey, maybe you're being too hard on her. You don't know that she used that kid. You don't know what happened after she left; you don't know what lead to Pierce's suicide and you don't know if Liz had anything to do with it."

She was right, Jack thought. He didn't know any of that.

"And you're being much too hard on yourself as well. Don't make decisions that will cost you your job, just to punish someone who doesn't need to be punished."

Everything Lorna said made sense. He was making very harsh judgments without facts, and one fact that seemed to strongly refute his instinct. Still, his instinct didn't usually fail him. "And if it turns out she did use Montgomery?" he asked.

"If you believe that, you fight her no matter what." Lorna's voice choked.

Jack was used to a composed Lorna. Her voice seldom betrayed emotion. The conviction in her voice riveted him.

Lorna cleared her throat. "If people are only about money, they're animals. You're not, Jack. You're a man. If they pull you down, you're no good to anyone—to me, to Ian or even yourself."

Jack Kendrick was a man of words, but now he had none; he wanted none. Gratitude flooded from his belly in a rush. It consumed him. He couldn't explain it and didn't need to. This pretty woman with the still manner understood, and seemed unafraid. She wanted nothing more of him than that he do right.

He reached toward her and she placed her hand in his, and they sat together in the still cool night.

CHAPTER 18

Squeeze Play

THE BOARD wasn't open when Jack arrived, but the early birds had already arrived. He hung his suit coat on the hanger behind his door. A hefty brown envelope on top of yesterday afternoon's mail pulled the entire stack precariously toward the edge of the desk. The San Bernardino County Sheriff's Department label caught Jack's eye as he picked it up. He slit the end and pulled out the pathology report.

The gory description under Cause of Death—"Impact of the engine, driven through the firewall...separated upper body pushed into back seat..."—kept Jack rooted as he forced himself on to the Toxicology Section. Just as Deputy Woodward had said, "Blood alcohol 0.08 percent." Below that a category labeled Anomalous Findings—"Traces of semen in upper and lower GI tract"—ended his reading.

Jesus, that answers one of Lorna's questions. Jack threw the report on the floor. Coffee. I need a cup. He walked out and across the office.

Irene stood by the front desk. She wore a yellow cotton summer dress with a full skirt that, despite Jack's somber mood, made him wish he could catch her with the sunlight behind her.

"Good morning, Jack," she said with enough enthusiasm that he was sure she meant it.

"Hi, Irene. You look pretty today."

"Thank you, kind sir." Irene smiled demurely and made a mock curtsey. "Do you have a minute?" she asked.

"Walk with me while I get a cup of coffee."

She followed him around the corner to the break room where a fresh pot of coffee steamed.

Jack grabbed a styrofoam cup, filled it, and sat down at the round formica lunch table. "What's on your mind?" he asked.

"Just to thank you."

"Thank me?" Jack was perplexed. "For what?"

"The new job."

"I'd like to take the credit, Irene," Jack said, "but you getting promoted off the switchboard was really Miles' doing."

"You don't want just a teeny weenie bit of the credit?" she asked.

"Irene, I agreed to it. That was all. I take it you're enjoying yourself."

"So far it's just typing and filing and returning phone calls for Liz, but she has some wonderful plans that represent real growth for me."

"Like what?" Jack asked.

"She's going to let me get involved in some of her accounts directly. Working with clients." Irene's face was full of excitement. "For starters—" Irene paused in mid sentence. "Liz told me to keep this absolutely confidential, but you're the boss. It's okay to tell you."

Jack instantly became attentive.

"She's going to have me work on the NCB account as soon as we get the listing," Irene continued. "Yesterday she had me doing some work for the presentation. She's sure we'll get it and says we'll be working on it for a couple of years."

"Probably true," Jack interjected. Just like her to start working on a presentation she doesn't know for sure she'll make. Can't accuse Liz of not being positive or prepared.

"Liz is going to introduce me to Pete Mastrionni over dinner."

Jack lowered his cup to the table and stared at her. He felt his mouth hanging open, but somehow couldn't seem to close it.

Irene's eyes registered his disapproval. She tried to explain, "It's not really like dinner. More like a celebration after the contract is signed."

He couldn't utter a word.

"So we can all," her voice slowed down with each word, "get...to...know...each...other." Irene stopped.

Warning whistles screamed inside of Jack's head. It couldn't be a coincidence. Both of them. Pretty. Young. Vulnerable. Needing her. Clients she needed to control. Dinner. Drinks.

"Young lady," Jack spoke firmly, "you hear this. You will not—NOT—under any circumstances leave this office to do any work for Liz Peterson."

Wide eyed, Irene pushed her chair back from the edge of the table. "Jack. Jack. Easy."

"If you do, you're fired. Do I make myself perfectly clear?" Jack demanded. "Do I?"

Irene's blinking eyes seemed to take up most of her face. "Jack, what's wrong?"

Jack stood up. "Irene, this has nothing to do with you. For now find Paul Jensen and have him come to my office. I'll explain later."

Jack stormed to his desk and dialed Dick Thompson. "Glad I caught you."

"Hi, buddy. I was thinkin' this might be you. Presentation's tomorrow and you promised to let me know who would be making it."

"And this is the call." Jack struggled to keep his voice at its usual timbre. "You're gonna get three of us. Paul and Brent Jensen and me."

There was a moment of silence on Thompson's end of the line. "That's fine by me. But you know that Pete will be disappointed. He's worked a lot with Liz."

"And she's a fine broker. But the Jensens are too. I think we can show him that. And I'm gonna dance with them what brung me, as Bum Phillips was fond of saying."

"Okay, buddy. It's your call," Thompson said. "See you at Pete's office tomorrow."

Jack looked up to see Paul Jensen staring at him. "So now I know what you wanted to see me about. What made you change your mind?"

"An old football coach," Jack answered. "Get hold of Brent, clear your schedules, and block off one of the conference rooms. I'm going to spend the day teaching an old dog new tricks." Jack paused, "I'll join you in a bit. Right now I need to have a chat." He picked up the phone and dialed Liz's extension.

*　*　*

A perfunctory knock caused him to look up. Liz wore a dove grey suit, black pumps and a self-satisfied smile. Jack found his eyes trailing the white silk scarf that looped around her neck before disappearing into her lapelless jacket. "You've reached a decision," she stated.

Jack motioned her into the chair across his desk. "Yeah, Liz, I have."

She sat. Jack remained silent.

"Are you going to share it with me?" she asked with a hint of a smile on her thin lips.

"I made my decision three weeks ago. Paul and Brent Jensen will represent ACRE."

Liz's studied casualness disappeared and the lines that gathered in her forehead momentarily reflected her anger. "You'll lose."

"Maybe, Liz." Jack put his hands in his lap. "But if we do, it won't be because our representatives aren't competent or we don't make a fine presentation." He leaned forward. "If we lose, it will be because someone tried to subvert the team I designated."

Liz's eyes flashed. "Fuck off, Jack."

Jack started to rise, but she held her hands up.

"I haven't done a God-damn thing. One of my best clients took over a project and invited me to make a listing presentation. I behaved properly at every turn. If there was any question about the propriety of my actions, I reviewed them with Miles, and I resent the suggestion that I've done anything wrong."

Jack was so angry he could barely speak. "Proper, my ass," he whispered, his voice choked with emotion. "You positioned yourself into a deal for which I'd selected a team, and then you tried to make it right by taking advantage of a Managing Officer too weak to tell you no! You did it while my back was turned, but I'm looking at you now, Liz."

Liz's olive complexion paled. She shot to her feet. "I don't have to take this from you."

Jack sat back in his chair as the adrenaline drained from his body and the hairs on his forearms and neck lay back down. He let a small smile reflect his momentary satisfaction. "Liz, before you go, tell me something."

She glared down at him.

"Did you select Boswell's building for Vance?" Jack asked.

"Me? Of course not." Her voice grew cautious. "Cornblatt picked the building. He was the client. The client always picks the building, you know that, Jack."

"But you agreed," he continued looking up at her. "You thought it was the best building for them."

"Yes, Jack. I agreed. Why?"

"Even though you only got paid half a commission?"

Her mouth turned up slightly at the corners and she fixed him with an enigmatic smile. "Is there something wrong with half a commission?" Her fingers worried at the edge of her scarf as she tucked it further into its already secure position. She turned to leave.

"Liz," he said softly.

She stopped and half-turned toward him.

"I told Irene I'd fire her if she left the building to do any work for you. If you force her, I'll do the same for you."

Her eyes flashed and her lips pulled together until he thought she might actually show her teeth. She shifted her eyes from him, turned and left.

Jack logged in, brought up his contact manager and clicked W. He found Deputy Woodward's name on the list, highlighted it, pointed the cursor to Dial, clicked and put on his headphones.

"Deputy Woodward here."

"Deputy, Jack Kendrick," he said. "Can we talk?"

"Sure. Go."

"I'd rather face to face."

"Important?"

"To me." Jack added, "I'll drive out, if you can make some time later in the day."

Woodward paused. "I've got two tickets for the Quakes tonight. My wife would welcome any excuse to duck a baseball game. Why don't you join me—about seven-fifteen."

"You sure it's no imposition?" Jack asked.

"I'm sure."

"Great, but can I join you about the sixth inning?"

"I'll meet you by Jack Benny about nine."

"What?" Jack asked.

"Ten-foot bronze of Jack Benny in front of the stadium. Real hard to miss."

"See you at nine. And, Deputy…" Jack paused.

"Yeah?"

"Thanks."

"See ya then."

*   *   *

By the time Jack entered the big conference room, Paul was hard at work customizing his conventional listing presentation. If weight was the standard of judgment, they'd win. Over the years, Paul had collected documents that took two volumes to present. The property description had to be developed each time, but the marketing recommendations section always modified old work. He devoted the second volume to a twenty-five-year history of Paul Jensen's marketing successes. Paul had well over a thousand transactions on that list. He had sold land to developers and then represented them to sell or lease the buildings they built. He had done deals on most of the buildings in the market.

Brent was off getting photos to add to the package. They'd have to keep a secretary late to scan in the photos and otherwise complete the edits and bind the packages, but in the end, Jack knew, it would look good. He wasn't worried about the written part. He worried about the oral.

"Paul, let's talk about the presentation. You know the questions you want addressed?" Jack asked.

"Questions?" Paul's baritone boomed. "I'm not gonna ask; I'm gonna tell."

Jack sighed. "Okay, Paul, what are you going to tell them?"

"That I can get more money quicker for those little pups, than anyone else they're talking too," Paul answered immediately.

"How?"

"Here's how." Paul grabbed the Exhibits Section in Volume II and opened a tab labeled Industrial Buildings of Less Than 10,000 Sq. Ft. "There are over two hundred small buildings listed here that I've sold. No one else has that history." Paul dropped the volume, straightened and stood with his knuckles plastered against his hipbones.

Jack took off his reading glasses, laid them on the table and rocked back in his chair until his eyes locked onto Paul's. "They don't give a shit."

Paul blinked and shook his head. "They don't give a shit about what?" he demanded.

"How many times you've done this."

Paul removed his knuckles from his hips, replanted them on the edge of the table and stretched over them toward Jack. "If they're not impressed by success, they'll end up with some clueless, snot-nosed kid trying to bring in twenty-five million dollars."

"They may," Jack said softly.

"Well then fuck 'em," Paul snorted, his green eyes sparkling.

Jack stood and walked to the water pitcher at the end of the table. He poured a glass and extended it to the still glaring Paul Jensen.

Paul shook his head.

Jack drank. "You think that attitude will win?"

"God damn it, Jack. What the fuck do you want from me?"

"I want you to listen."

Paul continued to glare for a moment, and then the heat went out of his eyes. He pulled out a chair and sat. "Okay, I'm listening."

Jack pulled out the chair next to him. "Paul, you've been the biggest pig at the trough for over a decade, and it's killing you."

"What's that supposed to mean?"

"Times are changing...."

"Bullshit!"

Jack held up a hand. "Let me finish."

When Paul's expression eased, Jack stared into his broad face. "Times are changing, and the biggest impediment to change is prior success." Jack inched his chair closer to Paul. "Your successes are so big, you can't seem to get by them. And if you don't learn, you're going to get your ass kicked—regularly."

Paul stared hard for a moment and then exhaled back into his chair. "I'll take that water, if you're still pouring."

Jack did and handed him the glass.

"What do I need to learn?"

Jack smiled. "Only one thing. If you get that, everything else makes sense."

"What?"

"Institutional types are not driven by how much money a project brings. They're driven by their ability to support the decisions they make."

"And the fact that I've done this more successfully than anyone else, doesn't support anything?" Paul's tone sounded almost plaintive.

Jack jumped forward. "Sure it does. Prior success is a better predictor of future success than anything. But it doesn't cover enough."

"What more do they want?"

"NCB wants to be able to hold Paul Jensen accountable," Jack answered.

"I'm a salesman; not fucking God."

Jack laughed. "You and I know that. Shit, so do they. But they want to try, Paul, and you have to let them."

"Show me how."

* * *

After Jack exited the freeway in Rancho Cucamonga, he passed miles of new subdivisions; all constructed with stucco neo-Spanish exteriors and red tile roofs. In the faint orange glow of the high intensity parking lot lights, the Epicenter looked almost as new and sterile as everything around it. As Jack walked through the half-full lot, the stadium before him erupted in a sustained cheer. He quickened his pace toward the banks of white lights that stretched above the ballpark and opened at a ninety-degree angle before him, spreading down the foul lines. A faint bronze glow below the lights assured him that the statue stood in front of the main entrance.

"He ridiculed Cu-ca-mon-ga for years," Woodward said as he stepped from the shadow at the base of the monument. "'It isn't the middle of nowhere, but you can see it from there.'"

The cop stood half a head taller than Jack. His belly hung over his belt and spread open his satin baseball jacket. He looked larger than Jack remembered. "So are the city fathers returning the favor or turning the other cheek?" he asked.

"Not sure," Woodward said as he swung in step beside him. "Good game on. Unusual for single A ball, but we've got a nothing-nothing pitchers' duel going through seven." He pointed to a well-lit concession stand. "Beer before you go in?"

Jack nodded.

They stopped at a concession stand before walking up a short flight of stairs and into the dazzling light of the jewel-box that was The Epicenter, home of the Rancho Cucamonga Earthquakes. It was clean, new, with real grass and no more than ten thousand seats spread in two levels extending along the first and third baselines. Jack noticed a double line of seven zeros extending across the electronic scoreboard above the centerfield fence. Bill led the way to seats only two rows up from the field and halfway between home and third.

"Nice park; great seats," Jack said as he flipped down the front of his.

"Quakes comp the sheriff. My turn tonight."

"Well, thanks for sharing."

"So what's on your mind?" Woodward asked as he looked past Jack at the pitcher's delivery.

Jack turned to see the batter frozen in place, unable to get around on the pitch, and the umpire jerk his thumb upward in the gesture of a called third strike.

"Kid's thrown peas for over seven innings now. Be fun to see if he can keep it up."

Jack sipped his beer. "I read the pathology report."

"And?"

"Well, it filled in some holes."

Woodward grimaced.

"No pun intended," Jack apologized.

They both turned to watch the batter pop a weak foul ball less than thirty feet up the first baseline. The catcher got under it, and the scoreboard registered an eighth zero for the JetHawks as the Quakes jogged off the field.

When the burly deputy turned toward him, Jack added, "At least we know what happened after Liz left."

"That we do." The cop pointed to the thin left hander kicking at the rubber. "Talk about contrast. Look at him. The Quakes' big right hander only has a fastball. Lancaster's guy has everything but."

Jack watched the southpaw warm up with a curveball that started looking like a batting practice gimme and ended up diving into the dirt at the catcher's knees. He took a gulp of his beer and set it under his seat.

Jack looked at the big cop until he got eye contact. "Suppose," Jack speculated, "that Liz invited Montgomery out for the evening, and over dinner and drinks coerced him into having sex with Cornblatt. And suppose Pierce so disgusted himself, that afterwards he committed suicide by running his Celica into the freeway overpass. Now just suppose that happened. If you could prove it, would you care?"

A soft crack caused them to turn toward the field in time to see a dying quail of a hit drop in front of the charging right fielder.

"Maybe, we'll get to him now." The big man's focus came back to him. "Jack, I'm a cop. Been one for a long time. Maybe as long as you've been in the real estate game. Over time a guy develops some instincts about his business. My instinct tells me that even if that happened, it would be real hard to prove. And, even if you could, while it would be of interest to me personally—'cause then I would feel like I had some resolution on the case—it would be of no interest to the San Bernardino County Sheriff's Department."

The batter got hold of the top half of a curve-ball and bounced it past the pitcher, but the shortstop darted to his left, grabbed the ball, stepped on second and then flipped it to first.

"Shit. Thought we'd gotten to the cagey bastard."

Jack waited. "Really?" he said when Woodward calmed.

Woodward sat staring at the pitcher. He sighed and turned so his concentration was on Jack. "Jack, seduction isn't a crime, unless the victim's a minor. That's why they call it the age of consent. And Montgomery Pierce would not be the first distraught lover to kill himself."

Jack exhaled slowly. "Thanks for the lesson, Bill."

Woodward jumped to his feet as the crowd exploded with the crack of the bat. It rose and sailed to the deepest part of the park. The JetHawk's center fielder turned his back to home and ran to the warning track. The ball's trajectory looked like it would clear the fence, but a few yards short it died and dropped into the extended mitt with a pop that Jack could hear from four hundred feet away. The partisan crowd gave a collective groan and then settled down as the teams passed each other exchanging places on the field. Again, Jack and Bill watched as the pitcher took his warm-up tosses. The JetHawks' leadoff batter took a few fearsome cuts at the air and dug in.

"Can that big right hander of yours keep this up for another inning?"

"Doubt it. The kid doesn't have a complete game since he got here."

As if on cue, a sound like a rifle shot exploded from the plate as the batter smashed a line drive, but right to the third baseman.

"One away," Woodward announced, sitting down before he fully rose from his seat. "Fortunately."

The wiry ballplayer walking up from the visitor's on deck circle stayed on the first base side of the plate. "This kid is so fast, he's the last guy we want to let on." Woodward was all concentration on the game.

The lefty let the first three go by, then hammered a two-and-one pitch over the head of the right fielder. It arced slowly toward the foul line, landed in a cloud of lime dust and jumped into the corner as the umpire motioned fair. The whole field moved in an exquisitely choreographed ballet, as graceful to Jack as *Swan Lake* and far more exciting. The JetHawk's third base coach pinwheeled his arm signaling the runner to keep coming. The runner responded by dropping his head and pumping his elbows hard as he approached second. The Quake's right fielder ran the ball down and grabbed it out of the corner. The second baseman charged to the edge of the grass in right as the third baseman struck a pose straddling the bag, glove hung low guarding it. The pitcher raced behind him to back-up.

As the runner rounded second and dug for third, the JetHawk coach signaled slide. The ball's flight stayed only momentarily as the second baseman took the cut-off throw and then accelerated as he fired it toward third and the collision that everyone who was paying attention had known was inevitable from the instant the ball left the bat. It all became slow motion to Jack as the runner and the ball raced for third, the runner in the lead and the ball overtaking him from behind. The Quake's third baseman prepared to receive whichever reached him first.

It was a tie. The runner dove headfirst along the outfield side of the bag at the same instant the infielder took the throw on the other side and swiped his glove around to the left. Jack, and five thousand fans, stared at the umpire's clearly visible form towering above the dust cloud that was third base. He slowly spread his arms, signaling safe.

"Shit, one out and a speed-burner on third." Despite his words, Bill's face hosted a wide grin.

"Will they bring him?" Jack asked.

"Hope so. Squeeze is my favorite play in baseball. Rather watch that than a grand slam."

"You would?"

"More drama in finesse than raw power."

The big right hander now threw from a stretch and watched the JetHawk on third with the same concentration a feeding pigeon gives a stray cat. The runner took a small lead and the third baseman held him on like a first baseman might. Shortstop and second swung a few steps toward third to plug the hole. The Quakes were playing it like they expected the squeeze—a suicide bunt where the runner starts with the pitch, the batter bunts and the run scores before the ball is even fielded.

Jack couldn't decide if it was more fun watching the pitcher and the runner play cat and mouse or Woodward anticipate the play. Twice the pitcher drove the runner back with a throw over to third. Finally, he came set and went into his windup.

The runner broke for home.

"Oh, Christ," Bill shouted, "he broke too early! They're gonna see him coming!"

Bill was right. The pitcher saw him coming.

The batter squared around to bunt, and the ball came flying—straight at his head. He ducked.

The catcher rose to collect the high, inside pitch and immediately dropped to one knee.

The runner never had a chance.

"Damn, I like baseball," the jubilant cop exploded.

The last JetHawk went down on three pitches. Nine zeros registered across the top line of the scoreboard. Eight across the line below.

"Now we'll find out if power wins over junk," Bill opined as he stood and stretched while the teams exchanged places for the bottom of the ninth.

"Something else I'd like to find out," Jack said.

Bill looked over his shoulder and down at Jack but said nothing.

"The building she sold him."

"What about it?" the deputy asked.

"Another broker had it listed."

"So?"

"So, she had to split the fee with him."

"Yeah?" Bill said as he sat back down.

The crack of the bat brought their attention back to the game in time to see the ball sail over the left field fence, and the fans rose as one, mostly to cheer.

"Power one; junk zero," Bill announced, and it was over.

They joined the crowd heading for the exits.

"She had to give up seventy-five thousand dollars to another broker," Jack said when they were shoulder to shoulder heading down the stairs. "And there were other buildings she could have sold him where she'd have made all the commission."

"So, if she went to all that trouble to get that much control over the buyer, why split the commission?" the deputy said. "Is that what you want to find out?"

"Bingo!" Jack said as they moved with the crowd past the statue.

"Well, only one of two answers." The big cop stopped and looked at him. "You're wrong about her, or there's some way besides commission to make money in a real estate deal."

The crowd flowing past the two men made them into a small island as the truth of the deputy sheriff's statement washed through Jack. It was there. He just had to find it.

"Jack."

The sound of his name bought him back.

Deputy Woodward's eyes held him. "Remember the busted squeeze play. If you try to beat her with finesse, don't let them see you coming."

*   *   *

Jack pulled the phone from the console and pushed the power button as he turned out of the parking lot and onto Arrow Route. It was late, but voice mail would do.

"You have reached the voice mail of Steve Ames at Inland Empire Title Company. Please leave a message at the tone." *Beeeep.*

"Steve, Jack Kendrick. I need a favor. There's a building I want information about—chain of title stuff—and I'm in a rush. The one Vance Electronics just bought from Max Boswell. As soon as you get the information, please call. Thanks, Steve."

* * *

Jack and the Jensens arrived early while Pete and Thompson were still at lunch. They set up their overhead projector, arranged their easels with selected aerial photographs, and placed chairs around the conference table so that the clients could look at all the graphics and still have eye contact with the presenter.

"I see you snuck in and got set up before we arrived." Dick Thompson strode into the room arm extended, exuding energy and goodwill. He'd removed his necktie. His white shirt was rumpled and the buttons gapped across his chest. Pete Mastrionni's thin form and weasel-like face followed closely behind.

After hellos all around, Jack invited the clients to sit at the end of the table facing the screen. He and Brent took seats along one side and Paul remained standing.

Paul approached the overhead and toggled on the switch. "You both know us so we'll skip the 'ACRE does all the deals' portion and start with the analysis of the project," Paul said as he put the first of his overheads on the platen. He spent the next fifteen minutes reviewing competing projects, prices of recently completed deals and an analysis of current demand. At the end, he concluded, "We think it will gross twenty-seven million dollars and take fifteen to eighteen months to get completely off your books."

Paul traded places with his son who was to review marketing recommendations. It took another fifteen minutes to cover four-color brochures, signage, advertisement schedule for local and regional newspapers plus the western edition of the *Wall Street Journal*, targeted marketing to firms in selected industries and cooperation with other commercial real estate brokers. Jack was relieved when Brent finished. He'd done a professional job, and if he'd come off as callow at least he'd avoided appearing brash.

Jack then stood to discuss any questions. He buttoned his suit coat, flipped off the overhead and said, "What do you think?"

The clients looked at each other for a moment before Thompson answered. "Good job. Compliments to the whole team." He turned and nodded at the Jensens, sitting side by side. "I like your numbers and timing, and your market recommendations are thorough." He stopped abruptly.

"I hear a, 'yeah but' in there, don't I?" Jack asked.

Thompson shrugged. Pete remained impassive.

"If there's a question, ask it."

"Okay, I will," Thompson responded. "We've heard from Grubb & Ellis, C&W and now you. All credible firms. All good presentations. Why should we think you'll do better than they will?"

"I'll tell you why." Brent jumped in, and all eyes turned toward him. He reached into his briefcase and pulled out four large spiral-bound volumes. He slid them down the table, two each to the clients. "You'll find everything Dad and I said in the first volume. But for now look at Volume II. Turn to the tab labeled, Industrial Buildings of Less Than 10,000 Sq. Ft. You'll find over two thousand—"

"Brent, I'd like to take a pass at this," Paul interrupted.

Brent looked quizzically at his father and slowly eased back into his chair.

"Gentlemen, just close those if you will." Paul nodded at the bound copies of the presentation. He waited until Thompson and Pete complied. "You can look at those later. You'll see I've sold a lot of small buildings." He stared intently at Thompson. "But that's not the answer to your question."

The clients looked puzzled.

He pulled an eighteen-column spreadsheet from his attaché. "This is the reason." Paul stood, walked to the end of the table, folded it open between them and spread it flat with his palms.

Jack pulled out a chair and sat down.

"As you can see," Paul explained, "this sheet represents monthly income and expense from now to project end. I've estimated how many structures we'll close in each month and at what price. Escrow and sales expenses are in here and will be accurate, but I've had to estimate property management fees." Paul looked at Pete. "You can put in the actual numbers for that item." He turned his head to look at Thompson. "I don't have any of NCB's internal costs, but I've made some estimates. You can adjust for reality. Based on recorded foreclosure information, my projections show a discounted rate of return on the project at a touch over twelve percent. Not something you'd jump into on spec, but not bad for a project you've had to take back."

Jack couldn't have been prouder if Lorna had just announced she was pregnant.

CHAPTER 19

Second Best

THURSDAY afternoon, Jack got the call.

"Hello, Jack." Thompson's voice didn't project its usual upbeat tone.

Oh, no. I've risked so much on this. Don't fail me now, ol' buddy. "Have you made your decision?" Jack asked with enough goodwill to mask his trepidation.

"Yeah, ol' buddy, I have." There was a pause, then Thompson continued, "You came second best."

Jack sank back into his chair as all the starch ran out of him. The consequences were too great. Duran had warned him, and there was no reason to think he was bluffing. This was going to hurt.

"Jack?" Thompson's voice seemed a long way away. "Jack?"

"I'm here. What made the difference?"

"It wasn't that you did anything wrong. You guys put on a fine presentation." Thompson's tone was reassuring.

"What made the difference?" Jack asked again, his voice softer than usual.

"Jack, we picked Grubb & Ellis. Pete just felt more comfortable with them."

"He didn't want to work with the Jensens?"

There was a long silence. "Jack, you knew the risk," Thompson spoke gently. "Pete preferred Liz."

"Yeah, I knew the risk." Jack paused a long while. "I'd hoped you'd trust me on this one."

"I'm sorry, Jack."

"I know this wasn't an easy call. Thanks for making it personally." Jack tried to lift his voice.

"The least I could do," Thompson responded. "Maybe next time it'll be your deal."

"Next time," Jack echoed.

*   *   *

Jack stood ready to kill, his feet spread, the shotgun tight into his shoulder, elbows pulled up and out at right angles until his arms lay parallel to the ground. He cocked his head lazily over the breech, looking down the length of the barrel with both eyes open and focused on the field of fire, the ivory dot of the front sight slightly out of focus in the foreground. "Now it's my turn, cunt. Pull!"

She came out running away from him, fast—flying to the safety of the weeds just out of his range. He saw her, a flash of white at the edge of his vision, and with the smoothness born of a lifetime of practice, swung the barrel until it slowly ran up behind her. Just before the ivory dot disappeared into the white of her back, Jack lovingly stroked the trigger.

"Take that, you bitch," he shouted over the roar of the 12-gauge as the clay pigeon disintegrated into a cloud of dust.

He lowered the weapon and unhinged it. The breech opened with a little pop and a puff that released the pleasant, pungent aroma of cordite along with the spent casing, which arced gracefully to the ground where it joined the growing pile of empties. Jack dropped another shell into the bore, snapped the Beretta back together and tucked it into the hollow of his shoulder. "Enough for you, Liz. Now for that gutless prick, Miles Preston."

And again he shouted, "Pull!"

He killed his enemies and his betrayers many times over. By the time the range closed at dusk the small mound of empty shotgun shells at his feet represented retribution to all of them. When he finished, his shoulder was as sore as his heart, and he had obtained no relief from his self-pity.

* * *

The porch light was on but there was no light showing through the plantation blinds that covered the front windows. Jack let himself in and stood in the dark. The porch light behind him reflected off the white saltillo tiled floor and stark white walls. It brightened the living room enough for Jack to see the cat, curled up on the sofa, open one eye and turn an ear toward him.

"Hi, Spot. You the designated welcoming committee?"

The cat responded by uncurling and then stretching, front legs fully extended and rump in the air.

"Yeah, I missed you too," Jack said as he shut the door and followed the shadows across the room to the kitchen where he snapped on the light.

Taped to the front of the microwave was a note. "Carnitas burrito from El Sombrero inside. Minute forty-five should do. See you after choir. Love, L."

Jack punched in sixty seconds, hit the power button and walked across the kitchen to the refrigerator. He pulled out a long neck, twisted off the cap and was back in time to stop the microwave before the annoying buzzer went off. He touched the edge of the plate to make certain the ceramic hadn't collected all the heat and then poked the end of the burrito with the same finger. Warm enough.

With the beer in one hand and dinner plate in the other, Jack took the stairs slowly, his arms extended for balance. As his eyes rose above the top of the landing, he saw a crack of light under the bedroom door halfway down the hall.

He used the bottom of the beer bottle to knock.

"Entrées."

"My hands are full. Could you open the door?" He heard the chair roll across the wood floor. The door opened as Ian rolled back across the floor to his desk. The room was in its usual state of disarray with books, papers, clothes and tennis gear hiding the surface of the massively framed water bed, spilling out over the floor and covering it all, except for a narrow path between the desk and the door. Posters from the Lakers, Kings and Rams, as well as assorted rock and roll groups entirely unknown to Jack plastered the walls. The ceiling displayed a massive hood decal from a seventies model Firebird. But the thing which caught Jack's eye was the newest item in the collection, a three-by-four poster of Traci Lords—clothed, if barely.

"Porn stars make the wall now, I see," Jack commented as he stepped into the clutter.

"Please, Dad. She's an artist," Ian answered. "And the most famous graduate of my high school. Got her start there, I suppose."

"I thought that honor went to the Smothers Brothers."

"Who?" Ian asked without sarcasm.

Jack shrugged. "Will you keep me company while I eat?"

Ian used his forearm to clear a spot in the clutter on his desk and hopped up. "I'll give you the desk and I'll take the bed. I don't think the other way around is going to work so well."

Jack set the plate on the desk. His son dove into the pile on top of the water bed and undulated back and forth with the wave he'd created. Ian rolled over when the wave action stopped and looked at his father. "You seem tired, Dad. Long day?"

Jack took a pull at his beer. "Long and disappointing. Lost a big one, I'm afraid."

"Sorry, Dad. Anything to be done?"

Jack just shrugged again and took a bite of the burrito. After he'd swallowed enough to talk he said, "That's not what I want to talk about. Lorna tells me your SAT results came back. How'd you do?"

"Pretty good. Not great, but pretty good. Total was 1175. Did better on the verbal than the math."

Jack smiled, genuinely pleased. "Eleven-seventy-five. Better than your old man by fifty or so points, if memory serves. I'm proud of you, Ian."

"Thanks, Dad. But I'd have liked to have been a lot closer to 1300."

"More is always better I suppose, but those scores with your grades should get you into a fine university."

Jack expected agreement but Ian said nothing and frowned a bit.

"Why the frown?" Jack asked.

"My grades may not be what you think this semester."

"You mentioned trouble with government. What's the guy's name?"

"Stratton." Ian snarled as he said it.

"Just one class? Is it bad enough to pull down your grade point?"

"Son of a bitch may give me a D," Ian spat out.

Jack took another long pull at the beer. "You want to tell me about it?"

"He's a prick."

"I'm sure he is. Now do you want to tell me what's going on?" Jack asked again.

"He and I go at it in class. At first he enjoyed it. Then he decided he wanted to be the boss. So now he calls my comments disruptive, and says if I don't control myself, my behavior will be reflected in my grade. He just wants to have it his way."

"That's his privilege, Ian. He's the boss," Jack observed.

"You think it's fair?" Ian voice registered his surprise and displeasure at his dad's comment.

"And I thought I long since disabused you of the notion that life was fair," Jack responded. "Fair doesn't have anything to do with it, Ian."

Ian looked sullen and said nothing. Jack saw a bit of himself in that expression.

"Ian," Jack said softly, "life is kinda like that. People in authority, teacher, bosses, cops, are in a position to demand that they get their way. You can buck them, you don't have to do it their way, but you have to pay a price." Jack realized he might be talking about himself here. "I got a dose of that myself today." He knew his face registered a bemused smile. "The price you'll pay is a shitty grade."

"So what price did you have to pay, Dad?"

Jack drained the beer before answering. "Aside from losing the account, I'm not sure."

"You going to get fired again?" Ian suddenly looked concerned.

Jack gave what he hoped was a reassuring smile. "It'll be fine, Ian." He paused. "What's important now is what you decide to do."

"Any advice?" Ian was less sullen.

"Depends on what you want. Do you want a better grade?"

"Yeah, of course I do. Might make the difference in getting my first choice of schools."

"Then I'd kiss his ass and ask questions that make him look good, and when you disagree either shut up or let him win. You might even try staying after school and asking his insights into especially tough problems."

"Is that what you want me to do?" Ian's voice showed his disapproval.

"What I want here is not important," Jack responded. "What's important here is what you want, and you said you wanted a better grade."

"Not that bad, I don't."

"Then continue on the way you are," Jack agreed.

"But then he's going to give me a grade that'll look bad on my college application."

"Probably," Jack responded and stuffed the last bit of burrito in his mouth and licked the tip of each finger.

"You don't care which?"

"Ian, I already told you what I want doesn't matter here. It's what you want. And you, my son, may have it either way you want it. It's up to you."

Ian's eyebrows pulled toward each other in a gesture of befuddled concentration. And then his eyes took on the luminescence of a new understanding. "But I can't have both. I can't do what I want and get what I want. It's one or the other."

Ian's words seemed to pull the stopper, and all the stress of the last few days drained from Jack's soul. In its place he was filled with understanding. The understanding that he had what he wanted—a family who loved him for his character. To maintain their love he needed to honor what they loved in him.

"Dad?"

Jack blinked and forced himself to focus on Ian's voice.

"Dad?" Ian looked at him quizzically.

"There are moments when it feels very good to be your father."

Ian lay on the bed, obviously pleased with his father's compliment.

"Ian, there's one more part of this, and in some ways it's the hardest part," Jack said.

"Okay. Tell."

"Be a man about it; don't whine."

Ian arched his neck and looked like he'd been slapped.

"Doing the right thing doesn't always get you where you'd like to be. But it's your choice. No one forces you to do it. So when the results are in, don't complain. It was up to you, and you got what you picked."

Ian relaxed back into the pile of clutter that was his bed.

Jack picked up his dirty plate and empty beer bottle and walked the narrow path that lead to the door. "I'll be interested to find out what you decide about your government class."

"You already know."

"I thought as much," Jack said as he opened the door. "Good night. I'm proud you're my son."

"Night, Dad."

Jack set his plate on the bathroom counter and threw the empty into the trash. He undressed and fell asleep almost as soon as he got into bed.

He awoke in the dark. Lorna's naked warmth pressed into his back and her fingers gently stroking his head. For the second time that evening, Jack was filled with the clear, self-satisfying realization that he had everything he ever wanted. Now he needed to make damn certain he didn't lose any of it.

CHAPTER 20

Come to Jesus

A SMALL mountain of paperwork overflowed his in-box, the residue of his total focus on the NCB account over the last few days. Today's challenge was to keep his butt in the chair until he'd whittled that stack down to size.

The ringing phone meant he didn't have to start just yet.

"Jack Kendrick," he answered.

"Mr. Kendrick, this is Mona in Mr. Duran's office. Mr. Duran asked me to call and tell you to join him here after lunch."

Jack's heart jumped into his throat. Certainly didn't take him long to get the word. "Did he say what it was about, Mona?"

"I didn't actually speak to him, Mr. Kendrick," she answered. "He was in Denver yesterday and is flying back this morning. There was a voice mail message from him asking that I call and set up the meeting. He must have called before he got on the plane. Will you be here?"

"Oh, yeah, Mona, I'll be there. What time?"

"Mr. Duran asked for one o'clock, but he might be a few minutes late. His plane doesn't arrive until twelve-thirty. He'll be taking a cab straight from the airport. If the plane's late, he'll be late."

"I'll be there at one," Jack said.

Jack walked to his door and closed it. He had four hours to prepare. That's four hours more than I had to get ready for Ira

Harkness when he fired me, Jack thought. But what's to prepare for a summary execution? The only choice is to accept or decline the blindfold and cigarette. Duran has all the power here. Unless...unless I don't play a power game. If I play a finesse game....

Jack picked up the phone and dialed,

"Good Morning, Inland Empire Title Company. How may I direct your call?"

"Steve Ames, please."

"I'm sorry, that line is busy, and he has another call holding," the switchboard operator droned. "May I put you through to voice mail?"

"Miss, this is urgent," Jack insisted. "Would you page him and tell him Jack Kendrick is holding?"

"I'm sorry sir, I have no way to page Mr. Ames."

"Damn it, go give him a message."

"Sir, there is no reason to swear." The operator's monotone broke. "I can't leave the board."

"You must have some system for urgent calls. Use it," Jack demanded.

"Sir, I've written a note and will give it to his secretary."

"Thank you, Miss." Now just don't cut me off.

"Hello, Jack." Steve's friendly voice came on the line. "My secretary tells me I've got to talk to you before you drive our switchboard operator to a workman's comp stress claim."

"Apologies, Steve, but this is important." Jack tried to stay calm. "Did you get my message?"

"Sure did. I looked into it yesterday, but there's one piece of information I still need."

"What have you got?"

"Boswell did sell the building to Vance, but it was a double escrow."

"Double escrow?" Jack stated more than asked.

"Yeah, simultaneous sales. One party sells to another, and the second party sells to the final owner, and it's all recorded at the same time."

"I know what a double escrow is," Jack said, somewhat bemused. "To who and why?"

"Oh, sorry." There was a small pause before Steve continued. "The county records reflect that Boswell sold a half interest to an outfit named Equity, Inc., and then Boswell and Equity sold the whole thing to Vance."

Jack's pulse jumped. "Did you get the tax stamp information from county records too?"

"Of course."

"So what were the prices of the two sales?" Jack could barely contain his excitement.

"Boswell sold half to Equity, Inc. for two million dollars, and Vance bought the whole thing for five million dollars. Looks like Equity turned a quick half million profit."

"Exactly," Jack agreed. "So who owns Equity, Inc.?"

"That's the question I haven't been able to answer yet."

"Why not?" Jack asked urgently.

"Corporate Filings Division of the California Secretary of State keeps a thing called the Statement of Officers list. It's on there, but I haven't been able to get it."

"Isn't it public information?" Jack pressed.

"It's public, all right, and I can get it, but it will take at least three weeks."

"How about if I go to the counter at the Secretary of State's branch office in LA?"

"No good, Jack."

"Why not, for Christ sake?"

"You're not going to believe me when I tell you."

"Try me," Jack demanded.

"They're not computerized. Still kept manually and available only on written request through Sacramento."

"Shit!"

"Jack, if you want to pay a private investigator, he might be able to pull the records in Sacramento and get them to you in twenty-four hours."

"I don't have twenty-four hours."

They were silent.

Jack drummed his fingers. "Would you fax me what you've got, as soon as we get off the phone? I'll go stand by the machine and wait for it. Maybe it will do.

"You've been a great help," Jack said. "Thanks."

"I'll fax all this over right now."

Jack hovered over the facsimile machine waiting for the documents to trickle out. It seemed like it took forever for them to print. He remained fixated, oblivious to the salutations of salesmen and staff.

Finally, documents in hand, Jack walked back to his office. He shut the door, fell into his chair and read all the details. He needed to be certain events had unfolded as Steve Ames described them. They did. He checked the math on the tax stamps. Steve quoted the prices correctly. They proved Equity, Inc. made a half-million dollar profit on the sale of Boswell's building to Vance. But who was Equity, Inc.? Who owned it? Until Jack could prove it was Liz Peterson, his squeeze play was busted. He couldn't go to Duran until he had proof.

Jack looked at his watch. Ten o'clock. He didn't have three weeks; he didn't even have two days; he had three hours. How could he move an intractable bureaucracy? He couldn't, and he knew it, but someone could. Who? Think, Goddamn it, Jack. Who do you know in Sacramento...Sacramento? Of course!

Jack dialed information. "State Senator Melrose's office please."

Jack scribbled as the operator responded and then he dialed again.

"Parker Starling, please."

"I'm sorry, sir, he's behind closed doors. May I take your number?"

"No, but you can take Parker a note telling him Jack Kendrick is holding, and it's absolutely urgent."

Jack held the phone, and for the first time in ten years, wished he hadn't given up smoking. The wait seemed like forever. A bead of perspiration formed at the back of his neck and ran down his spine.

"Jack, what a pleasant surprise. Viv said it was urgent. More urgent than tort reform?"

Jack chuckled. He could hear the nervous tension in his laugh and knew Parker could too. "Only to me, Park. But what's the sense of having old fraternity brothers, if you can't ask a favor?"

"Ask."

"Does the Senator have any clout with the Secretary of State's office?"

"If you mean state, not federal, the answer's yes."

"I do," Jack answered. "And can the senator's senior aid exercise a little of it?"

"Depends. What do you need?"

"A copy of the Statement of Officers list for a company named Equity, Inc."

"That's it?" Parker asked.

"That's it, but I need it now."

"Now?"

"Means my job, Park."

"Hold on."

There was an electronic click as Parker put him on hold. Jack switched his phone to speaker and cradled the receiver. He walked to the window and stood, his hands cupped in the small of his back. He stared vacantly into the parking lot for a long time.

"Jack?" the speaker popped.

He whirled and grabbed the receiver. "Yes."

"Equity, Inc. is a Subchapter-S corporation owned entirely by Tom and Liz Peterson."

Jack stood frozen, phone at his ear and leaning over the desk.

"Jack?"

He had her.

"Jack, are you there?"

"Yes, Parker, I'm here. Can you have it faxed to me, now?"

"Can do."

Jack gave him the number. "Thanks, Park. You just pulled my chestnuts out of a very hot fire."

"Glad to. Just don't forget on the first Tuesday in November."

"Not a chance."

"Bye."

Liz Peterson had done it. She'd sold a client a building in which she owned an undisclosed interest. She'd made a secret profit. That she'd violated company policy was the least of her sins. More importantly, she'd violated state law and Department of Real Estate rules. She'd lose her license. Vance could sue.

Jack wondered how she'd done it. Had Boswell offered her an interest to make certain he got the deal, or had she forced her way in? The District Attorney might consider it larceny if Liz coerced Boswell. Even without criminal charges, there would be a lot of civil suits. Liz was finished.

He needed to play this right. What had Deputy Woodward said? "Don't let her see you coming."

"Irene, would you ask Liz to step into my office, now?"

It took her fifteen minutes to arrive. Jack used the time productively.

"You wanted to see me?" Liz demanded.

Jack heard contempt under the studied indifference of her tone, but he didn't concern himself about it. He found he enjoyed watching her standing erect, framed in his doorway. She possessed the same sensual appeal he found in large cats. She was powerful and very dangerous.

"Sit down, Liz." She stood motionless. "Please," he added, and she walked slowly to the chair and eased into it.

"What do you want, Jack?" She stared into his eyes, refusing to back down.

She thought herself entirely in command. Jack knew better. Removed from the threat of her, he found real pleasure in observing the power of the beast. She was a predator, self-reliant, vain, able. A beast to be appreciated even if it had to be destroyed.

"I called you in to fire you, Liz."

She didn't move. She stared at him and didn't speak. Finally, she rose and started to leave.

"Liz, we can do this here, or we can do it in the open office, but you're through here. And if I need to call the police to have a disruptive ex-employee removed, I will."

She stopped at the door and stood with her back to him.

"Now close the door and come back in."

She did. After she took her seat, Liz leaned forward, her thin lips pursed. Her eyes burned. "You won't get away with this, you know."

Jack reached across the desk and handed her the pink copy of a multi-part form. "Here's your copy of the termination papers. I'll need your key, and then you and I will walk to your cube. You can pack your personal effects, and then I'll escort you to the door."

"This says, Moral Turpitude. What the fuck does that mean?" she growled.

"Wickedness, Liz," he responded. "It means wickedness. It means you went too far, and you blighted the integrity of your employer. Very old-fashioned concept. Did you know I could fire you for that, Liz?"

"We'll see if you can fire me. But for now cut the horseshit. What are you claiming I did?"

"You owned a commercial building and didn't divulge that ownership to ACRE. That's a violation of company policy. You did it; you're out."

"The Vance building?" Liz registered understanding. "Jack, if I failed to file the Notice of Ownership, it's not that big a deal. The client knew I owned a piece. Christ, Boswell needed my money to keep control of the building until we could get through escrow. He was under threat of foreclosure, and if it went back to the bank, who knows what the hell would have happened? Of course the client knew. I was doing it for him."

For a moment, he actually believed her. For just a moment, he forgot the half million-dollar profit. But only for a moment. "You're very good, Liz," Jack said, and he smiled. "But I'll stick with it. You're fired."

She rose and without comment walked out of his office. As he walked behind her, Jack couldn't help but admire the way the defiant set to her shoulders increased the graceful power of her stride.

When she passed the reception desk, Liz didn't turn toward her cube. She strode purposefully across the reception area and toward the front door. Jack followed. Liz reached the front door and swung the heavy glass open.

"Your key, Liz," Jack demanded.

She held the door with her heel as she reached into her purse, pulled out a key chain, and slowly removed one key which she handed to Jack.

He accepted it and held the door. She turned to look at him. A smile crossed her lips. It was the tight smile of a competitor locked in a closely contested battle. "I'll give that Notice of Ownership to the next manager who occupies your desk."

She left Jack holding the door.

* * *

Jack arrived at 1:00 P.M. As Mona had predicted, Duran had not yet arrived, but she ushered him into Duran's private office to wait.

Jack selected the chair at the end of the seating group and laid the large manila envelope he carried on the coffee table. He looked at Duran's personal trophies, which had escaped his eye on his previous visit. On the small bookshelf built into the wall Jack noticed

"Leadership Secrets of Attila the Hun." A black and white photo of a very young Jim Duran dressed in camouflage fatigues, with blackened captain's bars on the collar and an M-16 draped casually across his shoulder, stood behind his desk. He was smiling.

The door burst open and Duran entered the room, all energy and enthusiasm. He had a briefcase in one hand and a thick pile of pink message slips in the other. He tossed the case on the floor and approached Jack with cheer that belied his intent. He smiled. Jack recognized that smile. It hadn't changed in twenty-five years.

"No need to get up." Duran crossed the room and sat on the couch. "Messages. Too many messages. The one on top may be of interest to you." Duran rotated his wrist so the front of the message faced Jack. He could see URGENT printed across the front. "It's from Liz Peterson. Wonder what she wants?" he toyed.

Jack didn't comment. He wanted to let Duran unfold this conversation in his own way. Jack's turn would come.

"Well," said Duran as he dropped the messages on the coffee table, "I hear Grubb & Ellis got the NCB account, despite your personal relationship with NCB's guy." His voice lost all of its cheeriness. "That right, partner?"

"Bad news travels fast," Jack said.

"I warned you not to lose any more big ones, didn't I?" His tone took on an ominous edge.

Jack nodded.

"And I advised you that Jensen was a dinosaur." Duran paused for effect. "But you used him anyway." It came out as an accusation. Duran's voice went to ice. "Got anything to say?"

"Yeah, I solved the conflict that's bothered you so much."

"Oh, really?" Duran's tone changed to sarcasm. "How?"

Jack wanted the whole world to slow down now. He wanted to enjoy this, to savor it, to appreciate each expression, tone and nuisance and the reaction it achieved. "I fired Liz."

Duran stared. The smug smile left his face for a moment but was quickly replaced by an expression of contempt.

Jack pulled the top document from inside the manila envelope. "Here's your copy of the termination report," he said handing a yellow copy of the multi-part form to Duran.

Duran didn't reach for the document. He seemed to be contemplating which of several options would be best to end this. He opened his mouth to speak, but was cut off by a loud altercation in the outer office.

"Mona, I don't care what he told you, I'm going in there!" a woman's voice demanded.

Duran turned toward the door just in time to see it burst open. Mona's hand was on the knob, but her feet remained in the outer office as Liz Peterson pushed past her and into the room. Liz dragged a man behind her. He was small with very thin features and looked like a child being pulled along by his mother. He wore his black hair slicked straight back. He wore gold-rimmed glasses and a brown suit.

Liz came to an abrupt halt inside the door. Her hair flew wildly around her head, as she turned the waistband of her skirt to straighten it. Her companion pulled up beside her and adjusted his weight until he had his feet under him again.

"You're both here. Good. Has the son of a bitch told you?" she demanded of Duran.

"Hi, Liz. Nice of you to stop in." Duran's voice had regained its old cheeriness. He actually seemed to be enjoying himself. "Who's your friend?"

"This is my attorney. He's the guy who's going to sue your ass for wrongful termination, unless you tell this asshole he can't fire me."

Jack hadn't expected such a dramatic maneuver, even from Liz. This would be a whole new game of much grander dimensions. He stared, wide-eyed, trying to take in all three faces at once.

The attorney finally spoke. "Mr. Duran, my name is Joel Ballard of Nieuheigel, Crowl and Ballard." He held out his card. "I represent Ms. Peterson. I would advise you to take her seriously."

Duran reached for the card. "Mr. Ballard, I always take Liz seriously. Why don't you both sit down, and someone tell me what's going on?" He nodded at Jack.

Ballard took the seat offered at the end of the couch. Liz remained standing, her hip propped against Duran's desk. Jack nodded to Liz, "Tell him, Liz."

She looked at counsel who cleared his throat and said, "I presume you are Jack Kendrick."

"That's right."

"Mr. Duran, approximately two hours ago, Mr. Kendrick terminated my client from the employment of the American Corporate Real Estate Company. He is her Sales Manager, so I presume he has the authority to do so."

"That's right."

"His act was wrongful, and we are here to give you the option of abrogating it immediately or facing suit for wrongful termination."

"Wrongful?" Jack looked directly at Liz. "Let me tell you what's wrongful."

Jack pulled the autopsy report out of his file.

"Not that again." Liz spoke with a caustic edge on her voice. "I didn't kill Montgomery Pierce."

Ballard appeared genuinely horrified.

"Who the hell is Montgomery Pierce?" Duran looked confused.

"He's a boy Liz interviewed over dinner," Jack answered. "Just so happened they also shared dinner with the Director of Real Estate for Vance Electronics. Liz says she left them together. Boy got drunk and killed himself later that evening. It's gonna be pretty easy to prove that the Vance guy used him as a boy toy before he committed suicide."

"The coroner's report said it was accidental death!" Liz objected.

"I'll tell you what else is wrong," Jack continued. "It's wrong for Liz to obtain an interest in a commercial building without ACRE's knowledge and permission—a position she got through coercion, I might add."

Liz straightened from the edge of the desk to object.

"Oh, shut up," Jack insisted before she could speak.

Ballard motioned her to back down.

Jack looked toward him. "She told you it was an administrative oversight, didn't she? That Vance knew all about it. She just forgot to file the paperwork. File this, Liz!" Jack grabbed two documents from the stack in front of him and waved them at her. "This first one is a recorded sale of fifty percent of the Boswell building to Equity, Inc. for two million dollars. The second is a recording of the simultaneous sale of the whole building to Vance for five million dollars. Looks like Equity, Inc's. half instantly increased in value about half a million dollars, doesn't it?" Jack turned to stare into Duran's narrow little eyes. "Want to guess who owns Equity, Inc?" No one in the room said a word. "It's entirely owned by Tom and Liz Peterson. Somehow I doubt that Vance knows about that."

Ballard blanched and looked at Liz. Duran looked at her too, openly anticipating her response.

"Jim, I can explain that money...."

"I know, Liz," Jack interrupted. "It was just payback for the money you supplied Boswell so he wouldn't lose control of the building. Half a million dollars will make a lot of payments on a four-million-dollar loan."

"As a matter of fact, that's exactly what it was for," she snapped.

"Funny, that's not what Boswell says."

Liz inhaled sharply. She looked stunned. It was the first time Jack had seen that expression on her face.

"That's right, Liz," Jack continued, "after you left the office, I went to see him. Found him standing in the middle of his office all alone and looking befuddled. Not a soul there but him. Not even a piece of furniture. Just him and one single phone sitting on the floor. Seems he's broke. Couldn't make the mortgage payments on his remaining building. His lender's broke too. Feds have taken over, and they foreclosed.

"Liz, Boswell says you forced him to bring you in as a partner. Said you wouldn't let him see the Vance deal unless he did. When I left to come here, he was on the phone with a sheriff's detective telling his story."

All three men stared at Liz.

She sat down. "I…I didn't do anything…illegal."

"Not my ax to grind, Liz." Jack stood and stared down at her until she raised her eyes to meet his. "Montgomery Pierce was my ax. I've done what I need to, someone else can figure out the other parts."

She continued to look up at him. Her expression showed nothing but confusion.

"Time for me to go," Jack said. "Couple of things for you before I do." He handed Duran a stack of papers from the file he'd tucked under his arm.

"What's this?" Duran asked with honest curiosity.

"Copies of some letters," Jack answered. "One to the California Real Estate Commissioner with copies of a few of these documents. Then there's one to the San Bernardino County Sheriff's Department."

Jack stepped around the coffee table and started to go.

"Jack!" Duran barked, "let's talk about these letters. It may not be such a good idea to send all of them."

"Oh, these are just copies," Jack responded cheerily. "I stopped by Terminal Annex on the way over here. I've already mailed the originals."

As Jack walked to the door, no one said a word. He turned to Duran. "Anything else you wanted to see to me about?"

Duran shot him a fierce look, but didn't hold his eye and shook his head.

"No?" Jack gave a small self-satisfied smile. "Okay, I'll drop copies of this stuff at the legal department on the way out."

* * *

The mid-afternoon sky was clear blue, seasoned with little white puffy clouds. The small yellow ball rose until it disappeared into the larger yellow sun that blazed high overhead. From his seat in the grandstands, Jack lost sight of the ball. He lifted his hand over his head in an attempt to shade his eyes and follow its flight. Neither his hand nor his Wayfarers helped, and all he could see were bursts of light, as his overwhelmed retinas registered nothing but the overload.

Ian stood in the middle of the court, hand similarly extended; glasses gleaming back reflected light. Jack caught sight of the ball just before Ian's racket lashed out over his head and drove it into the court on the other side of the net. It struck with such force that its bounce carried it over the protective fence behind Ian's opponent.

"Advantage, Redondo." The speaker droned, "Match point."

Lorna grabbed Jack's arm with both hands. "Honey, he's going to win," she whispered.

Jack put his hand on top of hers. "Maybe," he said. "Maybe."

Ian slowly returned to the baseline, accepting a ball from a freshman acting as ball boy for the match. He juggled the ball with his upturned racket as he walked to his place behind the baseline. He turned to face his opponent and bounced the ball from his hand to the paved surface—once, twice, three times, as Jack knew he would. Then he tossed it high overhead, and as it descended, rose up on his toes and reached with the racket. At its maximum extension, the racket met the ball and fired it forward striking the service court deep and just inside the line. As it landed the spin caught and the ball jumped even further away from Ian's lanky opponent who managed to get only the top inch of his racket on it. As the ball wobbled back across the net, Ian met it and deftly dinked it cross-court.

"Game, set, and match to the new Ocean League Champions, Redondo Union High School," the public address system announced.

"He's done it!" Lorna shouted as she jumped up. "He's done it; they've won the league." Her eyes danced with delight.

Jack looked away from them to see the tennis team mob his son.

"Don't just sit there. Let's go down and congratulate him," Lorna insisted.

Jack reached up and put a restraining hand on her forearm. "Let's just sit here and wait."

"Why?"

"Now's their moment of glory." He nodded toward the tight knot of young men celebrating below. "This moment is for them. Our chance to add our congratulations will come soon enough."

He lay his head back against the hard metal plank two rows up, arching his spine to stretch over the row just above him. Lorna sat down beside him and lay her head on his chest. He closed his eyes, and soaked in the warmth of her.

"How much of it did you see?"

The voice came softly beside him. Jack opened his eyes and turned to smile at his son.

Lorna threw her arms across Jack's reclining form and around Ian's shoulders and folded his slim form to her. She kissed his cheek. "You were wonderful. I'm so proud of you."

"Would you two let me up?" Jack's displayed mock indignity in his tone.

They smiled conspiratorially at each other and then chorused in unison, "Oh, stop," and each put a hand on his chest to force him back down.

"Okay, please," Jack cajoled.

They again exchanged conspiratorial smiles, but this time disengaged their hug and let him rise.

"So, how much did you see?" Ian asked again as Jack settled between them.

"Lorna saw it all," Jack nodded toward her. "I got here for the last set. You looked good."

"Somebody once told me, 'On game day, you gotta be ready to play.'"

Jack reached over and tousled the blond head rising above his. "Who'd feed a young man platitudes?"

"Some old guy who can't anymore," Ian smiled and laid his arm over Jack's shoulder.

"Congratulations. I couldn't be prouder of you." Jack meant it.

"Yeah, you could."

Jack pulled himself up until his eyes were almost level with Ian's. "What did you do?"

"Solved my problem with Stratton."

Jack worked at keeping his face devoid of expression. "You get on his good side?"

"You know better than that."

Jack openly appraised Ian's face. He couldn't read it. "Tell."

Ian's face lit up with pleasure. "Kinda hard to give a D to the only guy in class who maxed the final."

Jack put one arm over Ian's shoulder and the other around Lorna. They sat in the bleachers, arm in arm, watching the afternoon sun settle toward the Pacific.

CHAPTER 21

Of Marlin and Morality

JACK SIGHTED down the length of the pool cue. All I have to do is slide it past Mike's six ball, and let it bounce off the side rail and back across the table. Put a little low left English on the cue ball just to keep it out of the way. "Eight ball; side pocket."

"No fucking way," Mike bellowed.

Jack stayed low over the cue, but raised his eyes to his opponent. "Eight ball; side pocket."

"This isn't the Beverly Hills Billiards Parlor, asshole." Mike Grazlyn grinned down at him. "This is Ercole's, remember? We had to put a quarter in the fucking machine to play. Even if you can line the Goddamn thing up right, this rail is softer than a baby's ass." Mike's sausage-like fingers squeezed the side of the table, and they both watched the rail give under the pressure. "There's no fucking way that eight ball is going to bounce true."

Jack laid his cue on the table, careful not to disturb any of the remaining balls, and stood up. "If I make this, it's going to cost you another beer. Care to make it a bit more interesting?"

"How interesting?"

"You've bought me enough beers this afternoon. Time for a drink."

"Call whiskey?" Mike asked.

"Call whiskey," Jack agreed.

"A beer on the game and a drink on this shot."

Jack bent over the table and picked up his cue. He bridged the fingers of his hand up, off the table, and stroked the stick just hard enough to gently propel the cue ball forward. It hit the eight ball at a slight angle and sent it into the side rail. As it bounced off the angle changed just enough to send the eight back across the table straight into the side pocket.

"Son of a bitch," Mike snorted.

Jack dropped the cue on the table and grinned at the big man.

"Enough," Mike added. "I'm tired of buying you beers. That's three in a row. I quit."

The two men walked toward the bar.

"My one satisfaction is that Ercole's has pinball machines and quarter pool tables," Mike said. "It sure as hell isn't going to have that unpronounceable scotch you drink."

"I wouldn't count on it." Jack looked at the approaching bartender. "A Corona and a shot of Laphroig for me, Larry. He's buying," Jack jerked a thumb in Mike's direction as he threw a leg over the top of a barstool and sat down.

"Another Coors," Mike ordered. "Do they keep that shit here just for you?" Mike asked as the bartender walked away.

"Me and anyone else who can pronounce it."

"Well, it serves me right," Mike said as he sat down. "I should know better than to bet against you lately. Liz did and look what it got her."

"That game played for slightly higher stakes." Jack swiveled the stool so he faced Mike. "But I'm not sure I know just what it's cost her."

"I keep up. It's cost her a lot so far and the price is still rising."

"Drinks, men." The bartender sat a bottle in front of each and a shot glass filled with a dark liquor in front of Jack. "Eight bucks."

Mike dug into his jeans and laid a twenty on the bar.

"Christ that stuff is expensive."

"Shouldn't bet against a man on a streak," the bartender said as he picked up the bill.

ALPHA MALE

219

Mike took a long pull from his beer. Jack sipped at the scotch. He could taste the peat smoke in it. He felt content as he set the shot glass back on the bar.

"You know, she sold that big house up the canyon in Bradbury," Mike said. "She hasn't been able to work since the Commissioner pulled her license, and Tom's income wasn't enough to carry it."

"That I heard." Jack worked to keep the satisfaction from showing on his face.

"And you heard about the RTC?"

"What about them?" Jack kept his expression bland.

"They're claiming the reason Inland Empire Savings & Loan failed was because Boswell couldn't repay his loan, and that he'd have been able to do so if he wouldn't have diverted half a million dollars to Liz."

"So where does that leave her?" Jack again picked up the shot glass and sipped at the dark musky scotch.

"Trying to negotiate to give the money back with no admission of wrong-doing. From what I hear, the RTC isn't going for it. Looks like they'll ask a federal prosecutor to press criminal fraud charges."

Jack arched an eyebrow. "That I hadn't heard."

"On top of that, Boswell's gotten on the bandwagon and is suing Liz too. Says she lied to him."

"Imagine that. Liz lying." Jack couldn't help gloating just a bit.

"It'll be years and millions of dollars in settlements, penalties and legal fees before she's through. She won't have a pot to piss in by the time they're done."

"Good!" Jack's expression turned hard. He drained the remainder of the shot.

Mike turned and studied him for a moment. "Why'd you do it, Jack?"

Jack peered into the empty shot glass as though there was something to see there. "Do what?"

"Change your mind. Why'd you change your mind?"

Jack looked up and smiled. "Let's get out of here. Ian's got a tennis match at three; I'd like to watch. We can talk as we walk back to your place."

"Not gonna drink that beer?"

"Three beers and a shot before mid afternoon?" Jack responded. "I drink that beer and it's time for me to check into Betty Ford."

Mike shrugged his big shoulders, and the two men worked their way past the jukebox and out into the bright sunlight. They rounded the corner and walked the short block down to the beach, and then turned up the Strand toward Mike's place.

All the students and tourists had gone, but the beach was full of locals. Jack saw a straight-down spike at the volleyball court in front of them and gave a low whistle of appreciation.

Mike turned to see what had caused Jack's whistle. "Teenie bopper?"

Jack pointed to the volleyball game in progress. "No. Spike."

Mike moved out of the way of an oncoming skateboarder and pinned Jack with an exaggerated look of disgust. "You are getting old."

Jack didn't respond, and the two men strolled in silence along the concrete walk bordering the beach.

Mike broke the silence. "So what made you change your mind?"

"Which time?" Jack looked at his friend and gave a self-deprecating grin.

"Jesus, it's tough to get an answer out of you. Why'd you decide to go back to the Jensens—asshole?"

"Wolves," Jack answered.

"Wolves?" Mike looked genuinely perplexed. "What the fuck are you talking about?"

Mike's confusion made Jack smile in spite of himself. "When I told Brent Jensen that I was going to replace them with Liz, he went into this long harangue about the social structure of wolf packs."

"Oh, Christ," Mike injected. "I've heard that story from him. All that Alpha Male shit. You didn't buy that crap, did you?" His eyes followed a young woman walking past. "It should be illegal for bikini tops to be sold in day-glo colors."

"Why not, and I agree," Jack answered.

"Whatta ya mean, why not? C'mon, Jack, we all get old and lose it. Athletes slow down, movie stars get wrinkles and sag, and us business types lose our hunger and the edge that goes with it. So what? So the old top dog loses. 'The king is dead. Long live the king.' That's what I say."

"Don't disagree," Jack said. "Oh, here we are. Casa Grazlyn."

They turned up the walk beside Mike's house and toward the garage in the rear.

"Brent's analogy doesn't apply to human prowess," Jack continued. "You're right. No one stays on top forever. Things change. The best today isn't the best tomorrow. But it does apply to human character."

The garage doors were open and Jack's Blazer parked in one of the stalls. They walked toward it.

"Character," Mike grunted. "How the wolves gonna tear down your character?"

Jack opened the door of the Blazer, and stepped onto the running board. "Seems to me, that a man lives by whatever standards he sets for himself. But whatever they are, he's tempted in a lot of ways to compromise them. And best as I can tell, every damn one of those temptations comes from another member of whatever pack it is he runs with. Those are battles a man can't afford to lose."

Mike arched an eyebrow. "Why not?"

"Sometimes they're little bitty compromises; sometimes big ones. Net results all the same. A man who doesn't have the moral courage to live by whatever rules he sets for himself, isn't much of a man, and sure as hell is in no position to lead anyone else. Every time he loses one of those battles, he's pulled a bit lower. I was just trying to stay on top."

"So you risked your job, for what? Just 'cause Liz didn't play by the rules?" Mike looked up at him. "I don't get it."

"Oh, you get it all right." Jack pointed through the garage to the world record Marlin hanging on the back wall. "You haven't cut the bill off that thing, so you can get it inside."

Mike put his hands on his hips and thrust his chin forward. "Ain't gonna either."

"I know it's a character thing. Kinda silly if you ask me, Grazlyn, but you seem to stick with it." Jack smiled down at his friend. "See you at the office Monday."